Go Slow

a novel

Lee DuCote

Raccoon Bend Publishing
Benton, Louisiana

Go Slow

Raccoon Bend Publishing
Benton Louisiana

ISBN-13: 978-1-7377911-0-2

Editors: Jennifer Jacks / Alice Sullivan

In Publication Data
DuCote, Lee

FICTION / Women Fiction / 20th Century

Printed in the United States

To all those who are facing hard times, keep to
the heavens and you'll receive your angel.

Acknowledgements

My profound thanks to all the people that helped make this story come to the pages. I do not consider myself a writer but a storyteller. And with that comes many corrections from many eyes.

one

<u>*Finn*</u>

Finn slid a frosted glass of cold beer slid across the wet bar and glanced over the heated sand. Salt-infused humidity lingered in the air. There was little wind as the Caribbean sun beamed down on The Split, the part of the island that separated the north end of Caye Caulker from the south. One thing Finn knew about the wind in the Belizean islands—it would change.

"Damn good beer!" A man held the glass toward Finn after taking a large gulp.

"Thanks," Finn answered, throwing a towel over his shoulder. Most tourists never knew that Finn brewed his own beer, and the glass the stranger was drinking from contained a new recipe he'd been working on during the summer months–the slow time for the small island located in the northern part of Belize.

Finn diverted his attention to the four girls who just sat down at the bar wearing nothing but bikinis and sunglasses. "Whatcha drinking?" he asked.

"What's wheat beer?" one of the girls asked, staring at the chalkboard menu that hung above the bar. Finn turned and poured four small glasses of the light beer that sparkled in the setting sun and handed it to the girls to try. "That's really good, we'll do four of them," the girl answered.

After pouring the beers and collecting their money, he turned back toward the table housing four taps and finished putting the clean glasses in a refrigerator to frost them. With the sounds of The Zac Brown Band filling the air, he thought back to when he saw them in concert in North Carolina, his home state. Finn was raised in a small town called Brevard, the gateway to the Pisgah National Forest and one of the only places in the United States that was defined as a rainforest.

The shrill voice of one of the girls pulled him out of his thoughts. "Oh my gosh! That dog is going to drown," she screamed pointing to a dark-haired ball of fur that was fighting the current that flowed through The Split.

Half the bar rushed to the sea wall and with phones out, began filming the dog that appeared to struggle swimming across the one-hundred-foot span. The other half of the bar chuckled over their drinks, knowing that the dog made the swim twice a day to visit his owner, who was one of the cook's upstairs.

"Should we jump in and save him?" Another girl looked back at Finn.

Finn glanced at the dog and then grinned. "Maybe you should just watch him and if his head goes under then you can jump in," he answered. Every time a tourist jumped in after the dog, *they* were the ones who needed saving from the current.

After the dog made it to the bar side of The Split, he shook off and gracefully trotted to the steps that led up to the restaurant. Two of the four girls petted him, obviously feeling sorry for him and his near-drowning experience. He ate up the attention and patiently waited at the bottom of the stairs for his owner.

"Drifters Reef!" another loud tourist yelled, leaning against the bar. He glanced at the wooden sign that swung from hinges on the front of the open-style building. "Where are the drifters?" He laughed.

"You looking for drifters or a beer?" Finn asked, trying not to be annoyed by the loud Canadian. After spending the last four years on the island, he could pick out the nationality of most people by looking at them and listening to the first three words out of their mouths.

"How about a dark beer?" the man asked Finn.

"Pale Ale or IPA?"

The man turned back to his friends who were still lingering around their rented bicycles. "We're in the right spot! This man knows his beer." He turned back to Finn. "Let's try the IPA. What brand of beer?"

Finn tilted a frosted glass under the tap. "It's mine."

The man looked puzzled. "You brew your own?"

"I do," Finn responded, as he handed the glass to him.

The man took a swig from the glass then held it up, examining the color. "Wow, this is good. Where did you learn to brew beer?"

"Family business back home," Finn answered before taking another order.

The four girls returned to the edge of the bar looking at the signatures and small notes that tourists had left on the walls and ceiling. They talked amongst themselves, pointing to different notes.

Finn handed them a black marker. "Just no profanity."

"Ah, you're taking out all the fun." One of the girls laughed.

Finn painted the bar every year, erasing the previous year's notes, signatures, and memories from those who visited. Painting the bar had become a traditional event that attracted the locals on the island, especially because of the free beer that Finn offered for helping.

One of the girls stretched toward the ceiling, unable to reach. "Climb up." Finn patted the bar.

"Seriously?" She smiled and with the invite, led the other three to join her for pictures.

"Finn!" A loud voice echoed throughout The Spilt. "This damn tap ain't working again." The grumbly voice came from above the bar.

Finn threw his towel down and jogged up the stairs.

B stood at the top of the stairs with her hands on her hips. "I told you that the damn thing can't be fixed!" she barked at him.

"It's okay," he calmly answered, opening the cabinet door to adjust the nozzle. "Try it now, B," he said. She might be four foot eleven but her attitude was six feet tall.

She walked behind the upstairs bar and pulled the level with success. "Still need to order a new one," she huffed under her breath.

B, as she wanted to be called, had come to the island for vacation when she met Finn and learned that he was looking for someone to run his restaurant. After spending the last thirty plus years in the business, falling in love with the island, and a native man, she took the job and never went back to the States. Finn had learned to accept her gruffness after he had three drunk tourists pick a fight with him and she single-handily whipped all three–with the help from a broken beer bottle.

"Who's minding the bar?" she asked as he emerged from under the cabinet.

"No one."

"Well, you better get your ass back down there before those damn tourists start stealing from you."

He smiled at her. "Love you, B."

"Go on." She motioned with both hands and returned to the customers who were watching them. As Finn jogged down the stairs, he heard her loving scoff. "Damn boy."

The Split was known for two things: Drifters Reef and the incredible sunset that attracted photographers from all around the world. A bell that hung over the cash register was sounded every evening as the last bit of sun could be seen. It was also rang when someone bought the bar a round of drinks.

With the sun on its final trek into the Caribbean Ocean, the crowd from the bar filed out to the sea wall, along with the dark, fluffy dog still seeking attention from anyone who would give it to him.

Finn wiped the bar down and leaned back against the sturdy shelves that held bottles of whisky, bourbon, and several different types of rum. He drew in a deep breath, watching the sun explode into different colors of orange and red. The spectacular sunsets were the main reason he decided to call Caye Caulker home.

With only the tip of the sun showing, he gave the rope under the bell a tug, ringing the day to an end.

two

<u>Sadie</u>

Sadie Barnet studied her packing list and tried to calm her every-growing nerves. Lying across a queen-sized bed with an abundance of pillows, Paige's dark hair spilled everywhere as she typed a text, while Sadie threw more clothes toward a suitcase.

Marking those outfits off the list, she walked into her bathroom adjoining the bedroom, grabbed her makeup bag, then went back into her closet. Who knew her small one bedroom in downtown Atlanta could house so many clothes?

A blue-patterned blouse landed beside the suitcase. "You're not taking this, are you?" Paige asked with disgust, picking up the shirt like it was a piece of trash.

Sadie stuck her head out of the closet. "Why not?"

"Uh, so last year!" Paige tossed it to the floor.

Paige and Sadie had grown up together as childhood best friends, and after spending four years apart while in school, Paige moved to Atlanta to chase her dream job and to live closer to her Sadie—not that they got to hang out much. Sadie's marketing job kept her putting in way over forty hours per week. But that's also why she kept getting promoted.

"I still don't think you should go." With a deep sigh, Paige fell back across the bed.

"I'll be fine," Sadie's voice responded from the depths of her closet.

"Who goes to the Caribbean by themselves?" Paige yelled back, a hint of mock jealousy in her voice.

Sadie emerged from the door, pointing a swimsuit at Paige. "Don't go there, I asked you to go, and even offered to pay for your plane ticket."

Paige sat up on the bed and crossed her legs. "Not everyone gets a *month* vacation a year."

"Two weeks . . ." Sadie corrected her before being cut off.

"Whatever. Two weeks of vacation and two weeks of personal time. It still adds up to four weeks which equals a month!"

Sadie turned to her full-length mirror and held up the swimsuit. "See, that college education paid off. You can add!" She grinned at her best friend.

"Why are you holding a one piece?"

"I just . . ."

Paige cut her off again and climbed off the bed, snatching the one-piece swimsuit from her hands. "You're going to the freaking Caribbean! You *are not* taking a one piece." She disappeared into the closet and came out with a two piece. Sadie tried to take it from her, but she quickly put it behind her back, which led to a wrestling match for the swimsuit. Paige fought her off and stuffed it in her suitcase.

"I'm not comfortable wearing that. It's too revealing." Sadie put her hands on her hips.

"You don't know anyone there. And if you're not comfortable, why did you buy it?" Paige spun Sadie around to the mirror and stood behind her curvy five-foot four frame. "You have a body like a pin-up girl that makes all of us jealous. Hell, it's all I can do to keep my hands off you." Paige wrapped her arms around Sadie's waist and playfully slobbered on her neck making loud kiss noises. Sadie screamed and laughed, but before she could loosen Paige's grip, she stuck her tongue in her ear, causing Sadie to laugh even harder, while wiping spit off her earlobe.

"I swear, Paige, you are the grossest friend I have!" Sadie grabbed for a Kleenex to finish the job, checking her sandy blonde hair in the mirror for any signs of Paige's antics.

"Oh, you love it and you know it. We'd make a great couple." Paige puckered her lips toward her, laughing.

Sadie started toward the suitcase.

"You're not going to take that swimsuit out." Paige raised her eyebrows as a warning.

Sadie crossed her arms, not wanting another round of ear licks. "I won't wear it."

"You are so freaking bipolar!" Paige threw her hands up in exasperation as Sadie pulled the two-piece out.

"How is that?"

"I have seen you at work. You rock it up there and are so confident. But you turn into this shy *Miss Priss* when you're away from your coworkers. Be tough and be yourself!"

"I'll be myself in a one piece." Sadie replaced the swimsuit and closed the suitcase, signaling the end of the discussion. "Aren't we meeting some people tonight?" She changed the subject.

"Yea yea, I'll text them," Paige answered as they walked out into the living room. "Actually, let me pee first, then I'll text them." Paige disappeared into Sadie's bedroom. "And are you telling Travis you are going?"

"No, it's none of his business."

"Well, he is your brother and has been taking care of"

Sadie cut her off. "It's none of his business."

Paige took the hint and disappeared into the restroom.

***

Sadie put up the dishes and folded her laundry before she finished packing for the night, finding comfort in a clean and tidy space. Dressed to go meet their friends for a farewell dinner, Sadie walked over to her sliding glass door leading out onto the balcony. Through the glass she could see the never-ending lights of Atlanta. Stepping out into the warm summer night air, the constant breeze from being twenty floors up blew her hair back, and after a couple of deep breaths, she heard Paige enter the living room.

"You good?" Paige asked.

"Yep, just nervous."

"Then don't go!"

"No, I have to. I need some time." Sadie closed the apartment door behind her and the two ladies headed to the elevator. Downstairs, the lobby was clean with light-colored furniture, creating seating areas that were hardly used.

The doorman dressed in slacks and a dark blue sports coat greeted them. "You two are looking beautiful tonight."

"Smitty, if you weren't married, I'd be after you!" Paige said to the older man.

He blushed then smiled and followed them to the front door. "Should I get you a cab?"

"No, thank you. We are just walking down to Randy's for drinks with some friends. I shouldn't be more than an hour or two," Sadie answered. Mr. Smith had taken a special interest in Sadie, having a daughter the same age. Knowing she was single and living alone, he was more of a dad than a doorman.

"If you need anything, just text me." He smiled, then turned his attention to the couple who had just entered the lobby.

The girls stepped out into the warm night air and turned north for the three-block walk. An early morning flight dictated a relatively brief outing with friends tonight.

In the early evening, the streets were still busy. Finally reaching the bar, an over-eager young man opened the door with a big smile and an invitation just waiting on his lips.

"Thanks," Sadie replied and before the young man could speak, two of their friends tackled them, pulling them back to more friends in a booth.

Randy's was a hotspot for a younger crowd of businesspeople and was normally crowded early with people catching a drink straight from work. "So, the world traveler is joining us this evening," one of the guys said as the girls walked up.

"It's not world traveling. I'm just going to Belize," Sadie bashfully answered.

"Oh, it's *just* Belize," one of the girls mocked her, smiling a genuine smile. "I'm so excited for you!"

Another sharp dressed guy joined them. "The usual drinks?" he asked Paige and Sadie.

"If you're buying," Paige replied.

He craned over the crowd at a waitress who had his attention. "A Manhattan and a water with lime." He looked at Sadie with a smile. "Are you going to drink water the whole time in Belize too?"

She grinned and shrugged her shoulders.

Paige threw her arm around Sadie's shoulders. "Don't pressure my girl into drinking. That's *my job*."

Everyone laughed.

"Now sit down and get ready," Paige told Sadie, "because I'm about to make a list of everything you have to do while you're in paradise."

"Oooh goodie," Sadie teased.

Paige stuck out her tongue and pulled up her phone notes.

"Number one: Swim naked."

"Paige!"

"Number two: Kiss a hot guy."

"Swim naked with a hot guy!" one of the other girls yelled.

"Oh yes," Paige typed. "That's going on the list. Along with a few other must-dos. And Sadie," she grabbed her hand, "remember, you only live once."

Sadie nodded. Didn't she know it.

three

Finn's boat rocked back and forth. Even with the windows fogged up as his air conditioner blew cold air inside, he could make out who had stepped aboard. His boat, a forty-one-foot 1989 Hatteras, had been tied up to the pier on the leeward side of the island for the last three years after he acquired it from a widower on the mainland. It had to be towed to the island where Finn had every intention to repair the two Detroit engines, a project that had been put on the back burner.

He opened the door to find a local friend, RK, standing on the back of the boat, looking over the side into the water. "You seasick?" Finn asked.

"Ha, funny. In order to get seasick, one has to be at sea. This old bucket of bolts probably isn't going to get to sea," he answered.

Finn smiled at the familiar jab from his friend. "She'll be at sea before you know it."

"Right. Not like I've heard that before. It's like keeping a bird in a cage. She belongs on the water."

"Okay, don't get all philosophical on me. Coffee?" Finn walked back into the cold cabin.

"Are you still drinking that American coffee that claims to be fresh?" RK asked. Finn held up a bag of Belizean coffee in retort. "About time. Pour me a cup. You have everything working but the engines." He shook from the cold air.

"I'll get them fixed," he answered.

RK and Finn had become friends shortly after Finn moved to the island. RK was as local as one could get, having been born on the island. After finishing school, he inherited his father's resort on the south end of the island. Caye Caulker had more than eight resorts. With two being American owned and built with extravagant standards, it was hard for the locals to compete.

"What is on your agenda today?" RK asked, flipping a bug out of his coffee.

"Well, if my sanitizer comes in today, I am going to start canning my latest batch of lager."

"Today?" RK expressed interest.

"Yep." Finn smiled before taking a sip. He had been working for the last six months on designing his first beer can, and with the help of RK's sister, an artist, he had come up with a rough black and white picture of his bar. He wanted to name his beer after his bar, "Drifters Reef" but felt that could confuse people, so he named it "Drifter's Beer".

They sat on the back of the boat finishing their coffee, watching the scuba diving boats carry tourists to the second largest barrier reef in the world and the famous Blue Hole. A small V hull boat drifted by with a local man paddling toward the open sea to check his fish traps. "Hey mon, when are you going to get a motor!" RK yelled.

"These are my engines!" the local yelled back, flexing his muscles.

The two guys were laughing when another voice from the pier drew their attention. That beer isn't going to can itself!" The guys looked up to see B standing over her bicycle.

"You want some coffee?"

"No, I have to make sure that damn cook cleaned up last night. Some of us here have to work, you know." She huffed and spun her bike around.

"Love you, B!" Finn yelled only to receive a wave back as she peddled toward The Split.

"Dude, she is one pissed off lady." RK chuckled.

"Nah, she's just putting on."

RK looked at him out of the corner of his eyes. "You sure?"

"Well, she's right. Gotta get going. Can you give me a lift to the shed?" Finn asked, throwing the rest of his coffee over the side.

The shed was a nickname the locals had given to the small out-building where Finn brewed his beer. It was also a place many locals came to try his beer before kegging.

On their way, RK dodged people in his golf cart on the unpaved road, and before reaching the shed they heard a loud voice coming from the hut on the adjacent side of the street that served breakfast. They turned to see the Canadian who was at the bar the day before. "It's my favorite bar owner!" he yelled across the road and waved like crazy.

RK slowed the cart.

"Don't stop," Finn said. But it was too late as the man jogged out of the hut with a hand full of mini donuts.

"You want some donuts?" he exclaimed, reaching the golf cart. Without answering, RK snagged two from his hand. "Kinda early for a bar owner to be out, don't you think?" The man smiled in curiosity.

"I have to can beer this morning." Finn waved off the donuts as sugar fell off the sides of them.

"Canning beer? That's something I'd like to see."

"Hop in." RK pointed to the backseat.

Finn gave him a funny look.

"You bet," the man said with excitement, sliding into the golf cart. "I'm Gary by the way."

"I'm Finn and this is RK." Finn took a deep breath, realizing he had just inherited a fan.

They rode the remaining twenty seconds with Gary explaining his small list of life's woes. He had missed his dive boat this morning. The air conditioner in his room didn't work. He didn't have any hot water. And his breakfast was under cooked.

"Sounds like you have some serious first-world problems," RK replied, stopping in front of the shed. "My place is on the south end of the island and I have two open rooms if you want to stay with me."

"You own a resort?" Gary was impressed.

"Hot water and air conditioning."

"Save me a room, I'll be down there today after I learn to can beer." He hopped out of the cart.

"I wasn't aware that I was teaching today," Finn said a bit sarcastically.

Gary slapped him on the back, causing him to fall forward a step. "Consider it free labor." He turned to RK. "See you later today." He pointed a finger gun at him, winked, and followed Finn to the door leading into the shed.

Glancing around the small building at the stainless-steel tanks, wooden barrels, and other small equipment, Gary said, "Man, not much here."

"It does the trick for me."

Gary picked up one of the empty beer cans and examined the artwork. "Who printed these for you?"

"A friend of the family," he answered.

Finn was from a large brewery family that had started off in Colorado before moving to North Carolina to open a brewery in Brevard. Finn had thought he would stay in Brevard and run the family business but after countless arguments with his father and a "cool down" vacation in Belize, he decided to relocate to Caye Caulker and start his own brewery. He'd managed to keep most of those details to himself.

"Do you mind me asking what you paid for these cans?" Gary asked in a serious voice.

"Why?"

"I'm in the printing business and print for a few small breweries in the Northwest." After Finn told him the cost, he said, "Let me check to see if I can beat that." He turned back to watch Finn start to sterilize his equipment.

four

As the turn of the century elevator ticked away on the way down, Sadie rolled her eyes as Paige continued to bend her ear about going to Belize alone. Sadie had never really done anything alone and loved having friends around, but this was a trip she hoped would break her out of her bubble. Her life in the last couple of years had become predictable and somewhat regimented, and she longed to be different, spontaneous, and had a deep wanderlust to see as much of the world as she could.

Smitty smiled as the girls stepped out of the elevator in the lobby. He took Sadie's bag. "To the airport?" he asked.

"Please," she answered.

"Smitty! Tell her she is out of her head to go to Belize alone." Paige tried to gain support.

"Oh, I don't know. Sometimes it's good to get away and meet new people. You aren't going anywhere dangerous?"

Sadie laughed. "No, it's a small island." Then she turned to Paige. "With *lots* of tourists," her voice grew.

Paige threw up her hands. "Fine! It was nice knowing you." She paused then added, "You know I'm just worried…with your problem, it's not safe for you to be traveling. What if you. . . "

"I'll be ok." Sadie cut her off.

Smitty chuckled and hailed a taxi. Paige dramatically squared up in front of Sadie, saying, "Promise me you'll text me every minute of the day . . . and night."

"Yes, Mother. And they have internet, we can talk and FaceTime," Sadie said hugging her.

It was still dark in the early morning hours, but the streets were filling up with people getting a jump on their day. Sadie opened the cab door just as Paige said, "See you in one month!" She held up a finger implying that was all the time she was allowed to be gone.

The cab jerked out into traffic and fought its way through Atlanta heading toward the airport. Checking for her plane ticket and passport one last time, Sadie took a deep breath and laid her head against the headrest. She closed her eyes and thought back to the pictures of Caye Caulker she had seen on the internet and pictured herself on the beach. A smile formed on her face as she imagined the heat of the sun on her skin, gazing out to nothing but the Caribbean Sea.

The cab came to a sudden stop. Upon opening her eyes, she realized they were already at the airport. *Dang, that was fast.*

Just like an anthill gets busy after being kicked, the Atlanta airport was filled with businesspeople jetting off to their destinations and families scrambling to their gates for summer vacations. Sadie paid the driver and started to roll her bag to the automatic doors when a man in a suit dashed in front of her, cutting her off. She drew back with eyes wide open. *Five hours, in five hours it will be slower.* She repeated this mantra over and over in her head. And like a small mouse, she zig-zagged through the bustle toward the counter to check her bag.

Forty-five minutes later after making it through security, the line at the coffee shop, and finding her gate, she sat picking the raisins out of her scone and sipping an over-cooked cup of coffee. A voice echoed through the terminal calling a few names, and Sadie looked up in surprise when she heard her name. She quickly made her way up to the lady standing behind the gate counter. "You called my name?"

"Since all the other names are men's, you must be Sadie," she replied looking at her screen.

"I am," she answered.

"This flight is oversold and since you are traveling alone, we need to bump you to the next flight to Houston."

"How long is that?"

"In two hours," she answered.

"No." Sadie stood straighter. "I booked my flight two months ago and I am heading to Belize for a month. I need to stay on this flight."

The lady looked over at the counter with an unexpressive look, studying Sadie and almost daring her to argue. "Please," Sadie said. The lady's expression changed ever so slightly, and with a smile and nod she looked back at the screen. Then with a few clicks, she handed Sadie a new ticket. "I really need to be on this flight. I might never have another chance." Sadie pointed to the door, trying not to panic.

"You are. First class wasn't full, so I bumped you there." She placed her finger in front of her lips. "Don't say anything."

Sadie exhaled and glanced down at the first-class ticket that held her name, then looked back to the lady. "Thank you." Her shoulders relaxed in relief as the woman motioned for her to board the plane.

"Enjoy your flight . . . and your time in Belize." She reached behind Sadie to take the next person's ticket.

Within ten minutes first class boarding was complete and after taking a selfie of herself and the ticket, she sent it to Paige along with her near miss at missing her flight.

Her phone buzzed with a reply from Paige. *I told you batting those green puppy dog eyes at people would get you places!*

Sadie giggled at Paige's reply as an older lady took the seat beside her.

"Good morning," she greeted Sadie.

"Good morning."

"Business trip?" she asked.

"No, ma'am, I'm taking some time off."

"In Houston?"

"Belize," Sadie answered, receiving a smile from the lady.

As people shoved their way through first-class, a man stumbled, causing him to lose his grip on the briefcase he was carrying, causing it to crash to the floor as his arm flailed between Sadie and the other lady, nearly hitting them.

"Are you okay?" the lady seated next to Sadie asked him.

"I am, thank you." The man shook his head from embarrassment, collected his briefcase, and continued back to coach.

The lady turned to Sadie who was now breathing heavy, holding her chest. "Are you okay?" the lady asked with concern.

"I am," she panted. "That just took my breath away, seeing him nearly fall." The lie fell from her lips, well-practiced since almost no one knew the truth about her health.

She closed her eyes and concentrated on slowing her breathing.

Changing the subject, the lady said, "So, what is a single girl taking time off from?"

Still fighting to calm her breathing and heart-rate, she said, "I've never done anything by myself and just felt like it was time."

The lady softly patted her leg. "Good for you, dear. That is something I didn't do until later in life. And something I have regretted."

"What about you? Business?"

"Yes, unfortunately. My husband died a few years ago, leaving me the business to run."

"Oh, I'm sorry." Sadie leaned closer to the woman.

"About him dying or me running the business?"

"I don't . . ."

The lady cut her off, laughing. "I'm teasing you. Don't be sorry, I get to jet around the country meeting people, staying at the finest places, and eating the best food. If I could get my son to get off his ass and take some responsibility, I would give him the business so I could do what you're doing."

"I don't know. My friend thinks I'm crazy for going alone."

"Guy?"

"No, girl. Although my brother would hate that I'm going. I decided not to tell him." Sadie gave a half-smile.

"Well, take it from someone who has been there and done that. Travel! Go see places and find you a good man. Don't live your life by the book like most people do."

"Thanks," she said. Just then, the stewardess handed the lady a bottle of water. Sadie took the opportunity to dig in her small bag and pull out her earbuds. She plugged them into her phone and focused on feeling her heartbeat slow down.

five

Finn locked the doors to the shed as Gary headed to meet his group of friends with two six packs tucked under each arm. A little mangy dog appeared from around a shop with a little boy chasing him. Finn caught the dog in the middle of the road.

"Thanks, mister," the breathless boy said, clipping the leash into his collar.

With lunch time winding down, island streets were quiet–with the exception of Gary's voice announcing to everyone about the new beer he was carrying. Finn's stomach reminded him that he had skipped lunch and knowing RK would be close to the surf shop, he headed toward the piers. Making his way down the main road, he nodded and thanked all the street vendors who tried to sell him lunch from their makeshift booths and fifty-five-gallon drums that had been turned into BBQ pits.

He turned down the beach road, which was merely a sandy path wide enough for a golf cart and caught a glimpse of RK sitting at a picnic table with another local.

"Did you eat?" RK asked.

"Waiting on you," Finn answered.

RK climbed out of the table. "Waiting on me?" He laughed.

Back-tracking to the street vendors, the smell of grilled lobster lingered in the air, drawing both men to a native lady who wrote down their order before they said anything. A few minutes later, arms full of lobster wraps, chips, and drinks, they slowly walked back to the picnic table, trying not to spill anything.

Neither RK nor Finn said anything, partially because they were stuffing their mouths and partially because they were around each other so much they had run out of things to say. Their attention was on the water as the roar of twin outboard engines and the blare of country music from a boat made its way up the beach. They watched as the boat grew closer with five bikini-clad girls singing and swaying, holding red solo cups in the air like they were on spring break.

RK shook his head. "I am in the wrong business."

The boat, with six paddle boards tied on the top rack, pulled up to the pier in front of the surf shop. The captain tried to tell the girls to stay seated, but to no avail. After the bow tapped the pier, all five girls fell back into their seats, spilling their drinks on themselves and on the inside of the center console boat. The young man tied the boat up, shot a glance at Finn and RK followed by a wave, then pointed to the girls that were staggering out of the boat, motioning too much drinking.

"Looks like a fun trip," RK said as the clan spilled onto the beach.

"For them," the young native captain answered, obviously knowing he'd have to clean up the boat later.

"Oh Toby, you wouldn't trade it for nothing in the world." Finn laughed at the young man.

Toby had lived on the island for the last ten years with his young and now very pregnant wife who handled the shop while he was out guiding stand up paddle trips. Toby rolled his eyes at the comment and went back to the boat for the remaining items.

"You know Toby?" One of the girls fell toward their table. "We love Toby!" She pointed to the rest of the girls speaking in a slur.

"I know his wife too." Finn nodded toward the small dark-complected girl who was walking toward the boat, her belly sticking out past her shorts.

"Oh my gosh, you're pregnant!" another girl yelled, and all five girls rushed over to her, feeling her stomach without asking permission. Thankfully, she didn't seem to care too much. Sometimes the costumers left her and Toby bigger tips, knowing a baby was on the way.

Throwing an armful of paddles in the sand, Toby asked RK and Finn, "Are we doing supper ~~tonight?"~~ this week?"

"Yep, B is making her jalapeño rolls," Finn said looking at Toby. "You two are coming, right?"

With a nod he said, "The wife is cooking something."

RK and his wife Tekka started a weekly potluck supper earlier the year before and it had grown into a dozen of the locals gathering, eating, and drinking Finn's beer.

"Do you need help?" Finn asked Toby.

"Nah, I just have to wash down the boat. I believe I'm done today." Toby started to walk off then turned back around. "You guys want to catch some waves in the morning?"

34

Toby had created a lucrative business carrying tourists out to a mangrove island and leading expeditions through local nature, teaching them how the islands grew in the Caribbean Sea. But what he had discovered just south on the reef was some of the greatest waves for surfing, something he didn't advertise, worried that tourists would take it over.

"I'm in," Finn answered.

"Me too," RK followed.

"Who is going to run the resort?" A voice came from behind them and with all heads turning, they found Tekka standing with her hands on her hips, just as pregnant as Toby's wife.

"There's my beautiful pregnant princess." RK smiled.

"Uh huh." She cocked one eyebrow then motioned for him to scoot over. "Who's watching the bar?" She looked at Finn.

"Bar? You have a bar?" one of the girls exclaimed, overhearing the conversation.

Before he could answer, Toby said, "Best bar on the island. And best sunset views. It's just down on The Split."

"We're going to eat, then we're coming to your bar!" she yelled loud enough for half the island to hear, then disappeared into the conversation of the other girls.

"Did I miss something or is this loud week on the island?" Finn said, which elicited laughing at the table.

"Sure you don't want to ask one of these girls to be your date tonight?" RK smiled.

"I'm sure," he answered, his eyes widening from the loud outburst of laughter from the group of girls.

"Well, it's about time you start looking. You can't stay single your whole life," Tekka said.

"Trust me, I'm good."

"You are now that you ditched that crazy one." RK laughed.

Finn nodded. His ex-girlfriend lived on the island. Within the first year on the island, Finn had been set up with a girl who worked at a coffee shop. They dated for nearly a year before she became overprotective and started accusing every girl around, married or not, of hitting on him. Finn hadn't realized her manipulation as quick as everyone else had, but once she crossed the line with B, that was all it took. You didn't mess with B.

"I better head to the bar before I get matched up again. A woman is the last thing I need." Finn stood up and headed to his solace.

six

Feeling the engines of the jet starting to throttle back and the popping in her ears, Sadie knew they were getting close. She took a deep breath and exhaled with a sense of excitement, nervousness, and relief that she was finally in Belize. The plane was half-full, leaving her a row to herself to stretch out and sleep. A ding sounded in the cab and moments later the flight attendant announced they were beginning their final descent and to turn off all electronics. She watched out her window as the clear blue water came into focus and the white sandy coast of Belize formed; creating a smile across her face.

Once the plane came to a rest on the tarmac, the flight attendant got back on the speaker to welcome everyone to Belize City. Sadie let the anxious tourists push their way through the aisle and out into the hot blazing sun as she pulled out her favorite pair of aviator sunglasses.

A flight attendant smiled. "Thank you for flying with us."

"Thanks," she answered pulling her hair out of her face to see the bright blue skies hovering over the airport. Shuffled across the tarmac and through a set of doors she waited with everyone else for the bags before heading through immigration.

"What brings you to Belize?" a dark completed man asked sitting behind a glass booth asked.

"Vacation."

He looked around. "Alone?"

"Yes," she reluctantly answered with a hint of embarrassment.

"Ok, be careful. Some parts of Belize are not safe." He stamped her passport and handed it back.

Part of Belize isn't safe. Which part? She thought about the information. Something that was new to her. *I thought this was a safe country*. Deep in thought, she pulled her bag along behind her.

"You need a taxi?" a large gentleman in a uniform asked standing near the door.

"Um..." She started to answer then remembered she hadn't changed any currency over to the Belize dollar. "I need to get change first, I mean, I need to get Belize money."

The man shook his head. "There is no currency change here in the airport." Then he saw the expression change on her face. "But this one time I can help you." He smiled and pulled out his wallet changing the hundred-dollar US bill into Belizean money.

"Thank you."

Pointing at one of the $50 dollar bills he said, "You give this to the taxi drive to take you to the boats. Remember Belize dollar is double of US money."

"Thank you," she answered as four taxi drivers rushed her.

After picking one of the four cabs, loading her bag, and getting in the back of a converted old Buick, she was off through the streets of Belize City. Old dilapidated vacant buildings littered the streets with a poverty-stricken country making her feel funny about coming here for vacation. A handful of barefooted kids played on the sidewalk with a couple of shaggy dogs and an old faded soccer ball. "What's Belize City like?" she asked the driver.

"Lots of crime, not a place to hang out," he answered giving her another second thought about coming here alone. "But the islands are nice and very safe."

Finally, the answer I need, she thought.

In the parking lot for the water taxi to the islands, she paid the driver, collected her bag, purchased her ticket, and sat down beside an old lady. Barely having time to tuck away her money she heard a man yelling, "Last call for Caye Caulker and Ambergris Caye". She sprung up and pulled her bag toward the taxi, wishing the girl selling her the ticket would have told her they were about to leave.

Once the man took her bag, he stepped out of the way letting her load onto a crowded boat. Looking around she didn't see an open seat and then a voice above caught her attention. "We have room here." The captain pointed to a few empty seats. She smiled and climbed the ladder joining the captain and a family that looked to be starting their vacation.

Moments later a deckhand pushed off the pier and the boat pulled away from Belize City with the islands on its bow. She pulled out her phone and snapped a picture of the captain with the island in the background then typed across the screen, ***I'm almost there***.

Sooner than she expected, the deckhand threw a rope to a young boy on the pier, then scrambled to the back to do the same. A voice came from below, "All for Caye Caulker."

Sadie stood up and climbed down the ladder realizing she was the only one getting off on the small island. The young boy helped her onto the pier and pointed her to her bag that sat by itself for her to grab. The small wheels on the suitcase bounced and caught over each board nailed to the dock creating more of a problem than she wanted for her vacation.

She made it to the sandy beach path that led in front of a few small places to stay on the island, some called resorts, some called bungalows, and others just a room. With the heat beating down on her, she tried pulling her suitcase, but the small plastic wheels dug into the sand making it impossible. A few people walked past her wearing backpacks and carrying water bottles, something she was wishing she had: water.

Out of breath and sweating profusely, she stopped under a palm tree and pulled out the piece of paper that directed her to her resort. Studying the map, she felt herself get lightheaded and realized everything was spinning around her. *I shouldn't have come. Here five minutes and my stupid heart is screwing up again.*

With her pulse racing, she looked around for someone selling water. Nothing in sight. A fear came over her until a pregnant shadow appeared in front of her. "You need some help?" She looked up at a native lady.

"I am lost and don't feel well right now," she panted.

"First," she reached in her bag and handed Sadie a bottle of water, "this island is too small to get lost. Where are you staying?"

"Anchor Resort." She thankfully gulped down the water.

The lady smiled. "Oh! You must be Sadie? My name is Tekka, my husband and I own Anchor Resort. I saw you had a reservation starting today." She reached down to pull Sadie to her feet and after swaying a little said, "I'll carry your bag, the resort just right there." She pointed to a blueish purple building within sight.

"You are my island angel," Sadie answered.

"Island angel? I like that." She led Sadie to the resort. "So this will be your heaven on Earth."

Sadie hoped so.

seven

Sadie fell into a chair in the small office of Anchor Resort breathing in the cool air and catching her breath. Tekka finished filling out the paperwork and running the credit card as Sadie looked at the historical pictures of Caye Caulker hanging on the walls.

"Do you want a bike?" Tekka asked Sadie.

"Bike?"

"It's a small island so most people ride bikes everywhere; we have them here for rent."

When was the last time I rode a bike?

"Sure, sounds like fun." Tekka went back to her paperwork. "Is there a coffee maker in the room?"

"No, it's behind you. Someone normally gets here around 8 a.m. and makes it. Plus, you have a water bottle in your room, and you can refill it in here too." She pointed to a water cooler. "All right, you are all set for a month here at Anchor Resort. You can park your bike anywhere here, but you better lock it up if you are anywhere else on the island." She handed Sadie a cable and lock.

"Is there a problem with theft?"

After laughing she said, "No, not at all. But there is a problem with people borrowing bikes. I think it's mostly those who've had too many cerveza's."

"So, a drunk problem."

"No, no. There is no problem." She replied causing a funny look on Sadie's face. "People drink, they get drunk, and either fall or borrow bikes. No problem!" An awkward pause fell over the room then Tekka started laughing. "I'm kidding."

"Oh." Sadie laughed.

"One more thing." She stood and a very serious look came over her face making Sadie a little nervous. "The island has a very important instruction, *very* important." She paused for dramatic effect. "Go slow."

"Go slow? On the bike?"

"No, go slow with everything! You're on island time now." She smiled and handed her a key to her room. "Remember my name is Tekka and my husband is RK, so please let us know if you need anything."

Sadie thanked her and stepped back out into the heat and bright sun. "Where's my bag?" she asked loud enough for Tekka to hear.

"One of our workers already took it to your room. You looked too tired."

"Thank you."

Sadie walked across the sand between the small shack of the main office and the deep purple painted building that hosted eighteen rooms all facing the ocean. A metallic green bike leaned against the stairs leading up to her second-story room.

"I left your bike there," a young local boy said greeting her at the stairs, pointing to the bike.

"Thank you," Sadie replied.

The cold air met her at the door and after shutting it and taking two steps she fell across the bed. After sleeping for what seemed like minutes, voices and laughter of girls woke her. Rolling off the bed she looked at her watch, it had been three hours. *Wow, I haven't slept like that ever.*

Pulling the wooden door that led to her balcony she stepped out to see some girls heading to a dock that led out to a covered area with two hammocks and a few Adirondack chairs. Six girls, not much younger than her, barely dressed in tiny bikinis, raced down the dock with one of them never letting up and diving in headfirst. With the cheering from the other girls Sadie smiled thinking about Paige.

Just thinking about you, I'm here, she texted Paige.

And after a few minutes of watching the girls swimming she disappeared back into her room and opened her suitcase. Digging through it, "Oh no you didn't!" She pulled out three bikinis and no one piece. *Paige, I am freaking going to kill you!* she sent another text.

Well hello world traveler. I take it you're looking for your one piece, Paige replied instantly. Sadie looked at her handful of bikinis. *Stop looking at them and put your butt in one and go to the beach,* Paige replied as if she was standing in the room.

You and I are going to have words when I get back!

You only live once.

Sadie smirked at Paige's response then slipped into one of the bikinis, slapped on lotion, then found herself on the dock. She pulled back her hair, taking a deep breath and looking at the water that rippled at the foot of a set of wooden steps. The girls were floating and standing in the water just off the front of the dock, not paying Sadie any attention until she took a step.

"Be careful the bottom step is slippery as owl crap!" one of the girls said in a thick southern drawl.

"Thanks," she replied laughing inside and wondering how she knew owl crap was slick.

"Where are you from?" the same girl asked.

"Atlanta."

"Oh, the States. We've met so many people from all over, I figured you were from Europe or some other country."

One of the girls splashed the girl. "Europe is a continent, dumbass."

"Whatever. We're from College Station," she volunteered.

"What brings you down here?" Sadie made her way into the warm clear water.

"Just had to get out of Dodge for a while. What about you? Are you by yourself?"

"Yea. And the same, just needed a break from a fast paced world."

"We're going to The Split this evening; you should come with us."

"The Split?" Sadie asked.

"It's where everyone goes to watch the sunset, and there is a kickass place down there called Drifters Reef." The girl leaned back and dipped her hair in the water. "Plus, there is a god that bartends there."

"Ooo, the bartender god," two other girls said simultaneously picking at the girl talking to Sadie. The girls sat in the water talking about their day and the soon-to-be-night, helping Sadie make up her mind about riding with them or taking her bicycle, until finally the girls climbed out of the water.

"What room are you in? I'll knock on your door when we leave."

"Number eleven." Sadie smiled and, after the girls headed back to get ready, she looked out to the horizon thinking about the vast distance that separated her from home. It was a scary thought but looking up at the clouds that took the forms of different shapes she fell back to her childhood when she and her brother would sit outside staring into the sky.

Floating on her back she spread her arms out and slowly breathed trying to stay buoyant allowing her hair to flow out in all directions. It was the first time she felt peaceful about her trip, her body, her being alone, and everything else that had occupied her mind over the last year.

The words of her father played over and over again. *Travel, meet people, and live.* The same words she had heard since childhood.

Now she was finally going to listen to his advice.

eight

A loud pounding on the door pulled Sadie out of the shower. "Yes?" she hollered.

"Room service!" the voice yelled back followed by giggling from the other girls.

Wrapped in her towel, Sadie opened the door and, before she could respond, the girls let themselves in. "This room seems bigger than ours. Do you have hot water?" one of the girls asked her.

Amazed they let themselves in, Sadie answered, "I do…?" She cocked her head sideways, wondering what she'd gotten herself into.

"I'm going to shower down here." The girl turned to the others, grinning.

"You don't even know her yet. Jeez, you're probably freaking her out," one of the girls replied.

Sadie laughed thinking back on her college days and her carefree years. "If you need my shower… mi es suyo regadera" she answered then turned to finished getting dressed.

Within fifteen minutes she felt like she had known them for years and loved hearing their southern drawl as they argued back and forth about some guy back in their hometown.

"Damn girl, you're freaking hot in that!" one of them said as Sadie stepped out of her bathroom in white shorts and a blue lace top.

"Thanks," she answered a smile lifting her face.

After arguing her point to ride her bike, the girls baled into their six-seater golf cart and, with tires spinning in the sand, they headed to The Split. Sadie was happy with her decision to ride her bike being thoroughly entertained by the six Texans ahead clearing the streets with their swearing, screaming, and laughing. From a distance it seemed as if their golf cart had twelve arms and twelve legs, all flailing wildly. Staying several feet behind them, she could hear all the remarks from the locals about the Texans as she made her way to the bar.
As Sadie pulled up to Drifter's and parked her bike, she took in the smells of grilled seafood, the linger salt in the air, and the sounds of the southern Caribbean Sea.

Walking closer to the bar, she heard an older and attitude driven server. "Damn! There goes the peaceful evening," she said loud enough for everyone to hear her– though her gaze was boring into the six Texas tornados piling out of the cart.

"Not much for partiers?" an older man asked her as she filled tea glasses around a table.

"Not much for woo girls."

"Woo girls?" The man looked at her confused.

Sadie moved to the end of the weathered teak bar watching everything unfold, doubly glad she hadn't ridden with the girls. At this rate, they'd be thrown out before they got a drink.

"You know, woo!" The server threw up her arms and made a high pitch *woo* noise, almost simultaneously with the girls *wooing* as they lined up at the bar. She looked at the man. "See! The damn word is contagious like a yawn." She rolled her eyes and walked back toward—judging from the clanking of plates—must be the kitchen.

A bartender, the best looking bartender Sadie had ever seen, greeted the girls, a towel on his shoulders and a smile on his face. His light colored hair blended with the background of the bar and his six pack abs bled through the thin shirt he was wearing.

"You made one of you ride their bike? Kinda of dangerous after a long night," the god replied.

"Oh, that's Sadie. We just adopted her today. She's from Atlanta. Finn, Sadie. Sadie, Finn."

Sadie felt half out of breath—*the bike ride or the bartender?*—gave a little wave from the end of the bar. "Well hello, Sadie from Atlanta." Finn smiled at her with a sparkle from his perfect white teeth. "I'm Finn. And that's B." He pointed through the door the grouchy server had gone.

"Hi." Sadie whispered, then clearing her throat, said, "Hi. Nice to meet you."

One of the girls threw her arm around Sadie. "I told you he was hot!" Her whisper was loud enough for everyone to hear.

Sadie looked at him blushing as he laughed.

"What'll it be girls?" He spoke above them.

"Shots!" two of them yelled.

Sadie's eyes widened. "Oh, I don't know. I really don't drink."

"You do tonight," the girl with her arm around her replied.

"Seven of the finest shots coming up." Finn turned to pour their drinks.

A wave of nervousness and middle school peer pressure swept over Sadie taking her breath away. The girls just recently accepted her, something she wasn't used to, and fear of *not* drinking with them caused a wave of anxiety.

They all held up their glasses and toasted to a never-ending night. Sadie put the glass to her lips and closed her eyes. *Here goes nothing.*

The liquid hit the back of her throat and she didn't feel anything or taste anything. It was as if she was drinking water, but one look at Finn, who winked at her, made her realize he *had* filled her shot glass with water. Sadie smiled and the motion of her silent thanks earned another wink, and then he turned to another customer.

Four of the girls let out another loud, "Woo" and after the older server yelled from the above balcony to *shut the hell up*, they all ordered beer and one by one walked to the water's edge.

Sadie waved them on, giving her time to thank Finn. "Do you want a beer? Or ginger ale in a frosted mug?" Finn asked.

"You're probably thinking I'm stupid for even coming to a bar since I don't drink."

He laughed. "I don't think anyone is stupid who finds their way to paradise."

"Well, he's stupid half the time." The cranky server appeared from the stairs. "What are you doing with that crowd? You don't seem like a woo girl."

"Oh, I don't really know them. We're just staying in the same resort," Sadie answered.

Finn leaned on the counter. "Don't listen to B. She's an old crab. What resort?"

A loud snap against Finn's hip stood him up. "What was that for?" He looked back at B.

"Don't ask a girl where she's staying. And don't call me old."

"I only asked because I wondered if she was staying at Anchor." He looked back at Sadie embarrassed…

"Actually, I am," she answered.

B gave a smirk, shook her head, and went back upstairs to the restaurant.

"My good friend owns Anchor. If you need anything just ask for RK."

"I met his wife Tekka today, sweet person," she answered as the girls started yelling at her to join them for the final part of the day's sunset. She smiled. "I better go catch the girls."

Sitting with their legs dangling over the concrete seawall, Sadie joined them on the end as they loudly discussed how to land the bartender.

Finally the sun dipped into the horizon giving out a breath-taking array of colors that couldn't be describe with words. *And this is the show I get for the next month,* Sadie thought. The Texans never looked up and never left their conversation, never noticing one of the greatest shows on earth.

And Sadie never noticed Finn's gaze watching her as she took in the sunset.

nine

As the island grew darker and darker the girls became louder and louder with each beer that was either funneled, shot-gunned, or just drank, making it easier for Sadie to hide her ginger ale. B, who had spent most of her time cleaning the restaurant, had all she could handle of the woo girls and stormed down the stairs announcing last call well before closing time. Finn just shrugged his shoulders at the outcry and poured everyone one for the rode in red solo cups.

Sadie held up her hand. "I can't ride my bike and drink at the same time."

"The police really don't care," Finn answered.

"No, I don't think you understand. I did good to get here without holding anything." She laughed.

"Gotcha!" He winked.

The main street that divided most of the restaurants and shops was mostly empty, only a few struggling tourists window shopping. Sadie laughed at the golf cart as they swayed from one side of the street to the other with the same number of arms and legs flailing as before. A steady breeze snaked its way through part of the buildings from the ocean, flowing onto the sandy street making for a peaceful and surreal bike ride back to Anchor Resort.

That all changed when Sadie pulled into the resort and was dragged off her bike by one of the girls. "I don't think so."

"Oh, come on. You only live once."

Sadie's eyes grew wide at the invitation. The girl turned and chased down the group running down the dock, peeling off every stitch of clothing.

Sadie shook her head. "If I only had Paige's guts."

The screaming continued for the next half hour and then the girls trickled back to their rooms trying to cover up but mostly baring all. Sadie, who was now on her balcony, softly laughed at them thinking that Paige would ride her down the road for not skinny dipping with them.

The moon steadily climbed into the night sky the steady breeze turned into a stronger wind, blowing her hair back as she stared off into the darkness of a vast ocean.

The rest of the night was pleasant with a constant buzz from the air condition that was over the two queen beds in her room. Cracking open her eyes, she couldn't believe sunlight was already pushing through the blinds on the window. *That was a fast night.* She rolled back over trying to fall back asleep and opened her eyes long enough to look at her phone and see that it was just after 6 a.m.

She laid her phone down and it buzzed with a text. ***Wake up!***

Balancing the phone over her she typed, ***I'm up . . . it's too early!*** She sent it back to Paige.

Are you having fun? Or have you not left the room yet?

Yes, and yes. She laughed then typed in the basics about her night.

After several misspelled words she made the executive decision that coffee was a must, and Tekka said they didn't open the office until 8 a.m. So after covering her bathing suit with shorts and a t-shirt she headed down the street to see if anyone was open. To her happy surprise she found one small restaurant, serving breakfast and lunch, open its doors.

Surely I can make it back with two cups in my basket, she convinced herself. One for now, one for later.

"Good morning, whatcha having?" A light-skinned blonde women asked in a thick British accent.

"Two large coffees." She dug in her pocket. "Where are you from?"

"England. That'll be eight dollars," she answered.

Wow, no savings on the coffee. "You have a beautiful accent."

Handing over the change, she said "Thank you." She looked around. "Are you alone?"

"I am. Just getting away for a while."

"I'm Lorene. I own the place so let me know if you need anything." She turned her attention to another lady glancing over the menu.

With no lids and coffee spilling everywhere Sadie pushed her bike back and leaned it against her building, glancing sadly at her now two *half cups* of coffee.

The sun tracked into the sky with the island becoming alive with workers and people walking along the beach. Sitting on the edge of the dock, her legs dangling over the edge, she noticed a few pieces of clothes from last night and shook her head, softly laughing.

The morning was warm and the wind had died down so Sadie peeled off her shirt and shorts revealing one the two pieces that Paige had happily packed for her. "Coffee and sun tanning, only in Belize," she said to herself.

A small boat paddled by with a local heading toward the reef, she gave a wave, thinking it was a long way to paddle. And, keeping her eye on him until he became a speck on the surface, another boat with twin engines came roaring toward her.

Standing on the front of the boat was a lighter skinned man than the locals, and as the boat came off its plane Sadie realized it was Finn and he was aiming at her dock. She quickly turned to grab her t-shirt but the waves had pulled it into the water, and was pushing it toward the beach.

"Crap!"

"Good morning, Atlanta," he yelled over the engines.

"Good morning," she answered caught off guard, not by him showing up from nowhere, but with his six pack abs and toned body. She bit her bottom lip staring in a daze.

He leaped from the boat to the dock. "You might want to pick up your legs."

She just stared at him dumbfounded. "What?"

"The boat." He pushed it back, keeping it from hitting her.

"Oh crap! I'm sorry." She sprung up.

"No harm, no foul." He tied off the bow to the dock.

"What are you doing here?" she asked trying not to look at his abs or the sweat that had formed on his pecks.

"We are here to pick up your Texas girls and take them snorkeling. Are they still in bed?" He started to walk up the dock. "There are a lot of clothes floating in the water."

"From last night."

He devilishly smiled. "Sorry I missed that," he joked.

"So you own a bar but take people on excursions during the day?"

"Just for my buddy RK. Get your stuff, we leave in 10 minutes." He picked up his pace heading to the girls' rooms.

"Me?" she hollered but he was too far away. "I've never snorkeled," she said to herself and once back in her room she shot Paige a text about the conversation.

Don't regret NOT doing things when you leave in 30 days! Paige sent.

Two bottles of water, sun lotion, sunglasses, a towel, and five deep breaths, then she locked her door and skipped down the stairs. *Just live*! The words from her father echoed in her thoughts.

ten

Finn stood by the center console, talking to RK who was behind the wheel. It also offered Finn a good view of Sadie, who sat on an ice chest in front of the center console. She was smiling, the wind blowing in her face, and the other six girls hung over the side of the boat. "Maybe we should gear back," Finn said motioned for RK to throttle down. "Don't want to chum the water for sharks."

"How come you're not green like the others?" RK asked Sadie.

Finn grinned as she explained to RK that she drank ginger ale all night. RK smiled and shook his head.

The canopy provided enough shade for everyone to get out of the sun and when the boat came to a rest, Finn started his "how to" lecture.

"Do you have lotion on?" Sadie asked one of the girls.

"No, I didn't bring any," she said in a pitiful tone.

Sadie pulled her closer and turned her around, soaking lotion on her back and shoulders and, like elementary children, the other five lined up for the same treatment. "Thanks, Mom." The last girl hugged her.

"Mom?" Sadie laughed.

Though the girls were sluggish, Finn was impressed with their athleticism and their quick grasp at snorkeling. Sadie followed Finn and the girls once they hovered over the reef.

"I can't believe the colors! The reds are brighter than any red I've encountered before, and the yellows seemed to scream with a neon explosion. How have I waited so long to see this?"

Between different colored fish and odd-shaped coral, Sadie continued to kick with the group. Then with a quick glance at Finn, she took a deep breath and dove head first, pushing her body closer to the vibrant colors. Finn watched her, making sure she got down safely until she was ten feet down, then dove down with her. Catching her attention, he pointed at a cave in a coral head with a small Mora eel that had its head stuck out.

They kicked to the surface.

She pulled the snorkel out of her mouth. "I can't believe how beautiful everything is."

"Welcome to my backyard."

Swimming alongside of Finn she continued looking at everything while the sun beat down on her back. Finn stole glances at her every time she looked down.

Another one of the girls swam down chasing a parrot fish and Finn spotted something that everyone would enjoy seeing. He quickly kicked down and scooped up an octopus that was crawling along the reef; the girls stopped kicking and clued in on Finn. The current pushed the group slowly as all the girls, including Sadie, touched the unique creature that climbed on Finn's shoulder.
But with one fast dart the octopus jetted back down toward the bright colors. Just as it reached its home, a large green eel shot out of the reef and with one swoop swallowed their eight-tentacle friend.

The screaming got loud. But the six girls hit octaves that only an experienced opera singer could reach—and through their snorkels. Finn's eyes grew wider than the octopus's eye's before it was eaten. "I think everyone on the island could hear that," he said to Sadie who was speechless.

"Holy crap! That is one bad Mama Jama eel," one of the girls took her snorkel out of her mouth and yelled to the others. Then as if nothing ever happened, they continued.

The reef that ran the entire distance of Belize also broke up the larger waves that the Caribbean Ocean was capable of making, and as the group got closer to the main reef, the water turned more turbulent. Sadie was glued on the bottom when Finn saw her get caught up on one of the girl's fins which must have pushed a small wall of water down her snorkel. She shot up grasping for air and coughing the salt water she had inhaled.

Finn caught her mask as she slung it off and grabbed her arm holding her out of the water. "You're ok," he said a few times trying to calm her down.

She wiped the water from her eyes and looked at him. "I need to get out."

"You sure?"

"Yes."

"RK!" Finn yelled back at the boat. "Switch with me." And as if they had done this before, RK had his mask and fins and dove into the water before Sadie could get out. Finn threw his mask in the corner of the boat that was being pitched back and worth and started the engines pulling them away from the reef. "Here." He handed her a towel and bottle of water.

"I'm sorry." She looked down at the bottle.

"About what?"

"My stupid damsel in destress." She was obviously embarrassed.

"Oh, is that what that was? I thought you were choking on water." He laughed. "You beat yourself up too much." He moved closer to the group in the boat. "So Atlanta, why are you here?" Finn pulled back the throttle.

"Do I have to have a reason?" She looked at him.

"No, but a pretty gal like you just doesn't show up on an island for no reason. Boyfriend problems?"

At first she looked appalled that Finn was prying into her business but then she shrugged. "No boyfriend. I'm just here for a month. What about you, what makes a young guy move to the islands? Girlfriend problems?"

He laughed. "No, father problems." He looked past her at the group.

"So, you don't like authority?"

"Have you met my manager B yet? It's not authority, I don't like micromanaging."

"So you rebelled and opened a bar?"

"Bought a bar." He smiled at her. "And no, my family is in the brewery business and I thought I would do better here at a smaller and slower pace."

"Wait, you make beer?"

"Everything sold at Drifters Reef." He straightened up proudly.

Looking impressed, Sadie nodded. "Well maybe I need to try one of your beers this evening," she replied.

"I tell you what, Atlanta, the first one tonight is on the house," he answered trying not to feel too excited about spending more time with Sadie.

eleven

Not counting choking on sea water, Sadie thought the day couldn't have gone any better, and in the back of her mind knew Paige would be proud of her going snorkeling. The cold water raining down her back in the shower gave her the relief she needed from lightly sunburned skin. She closed her eyes and dipped her hair back into the water rinsing out the conditioner and the vision of Finn without his shirt appeared like a movie.

After drying off, a buzz from her phone caught her attention. ***Well, how was today?*** Paige texted.

She sat on the side of the bed. ***Great! How was yours?***

Details! And stop worrying about my day.

I went snorkeling with the girls from Texas, she sent. ***And Finn took us,*** she added.

Sadie imagined that Paige sat up with that added bit.

Send me a picture of this Finn tonight.

Glancing out her balcony door she could see the sun still high in the sky giving her plenty of time to eat and then to The Split for sunset. A knock drew her to her front door and, opening it, she found two of the Texas girls wrapped in towels with smiles on their face.

"Shower?" Sadie asked.

"Please?" they both replied.

Sadie smiled back and motioned for them to come in. One of the girls dropped her towel to her side before disappearing behind the curtains.

"The college life," Sadie said out loud thinking about their free spirit.

"Do you have a boyfriend?" the other girl asked making conversation.

"No, you?"

"I think you should go out with Finn."

The statement took her by surprise. "Finn?" She choked on her words.

"Did you see how he looked at you today? You two would make a great couple. Are you going to The Split for sunset?" She spotted a small top on Sadie's bed and said, "Wear this."

Sadie shook her head with all the questions flying around. "Why do you think we would make a couple?"

72

The shower curtains opened with a head sticking out. "Want us to set you two up?"

"No. I thought the other girl liked him?" Sadie referred to another one of their friends.

"Oh, she thinks he's hot. But she falls in love with everyone," the girl on the bed replied like it was no big deal.

Later, with the thought of being fixed up with Finn racing through her mind, Sadie peddled out of the resort and onto the sandy roads of Caye Caulker. The first building she passed was a hostel with a full porch of millennials drinking, listening to a guy with dreadlocks play guitar, and just living life. Sadie had a hint of jealously at their carefree lifestyle and no fear to any adventure that crossed their path.

A little farther down a short local woman tripped, spilling her basket of groceries. The sound of rocks sliding on sand came from Sadie's tires as she locked up her brakes. Dropping her bike she helped the lady up and collected her things placing them back in the basket. "Thank you," the lady said over and over again grateful for her help.

"Finally, a tourist who gives a damn." A voice from behind her caused her to turn.

Sadie stood up. "I would hope anyone would stop and help," she said to Lorene, the owner of the breakfast and lunch place.

"You'd be surprised," she answered in her thick accent.

The lady tried to give Sadie an orange as payment for helping her, but Sadie smiled and refused, thinking that could easily be her family's breakfast. Lorene picked up her bike and wheeled it to her. "Thank you," Sadie said.

"Let me guess, you're going to The Split for sunset?"

"After I eat."

"Well, B is one heck of a restaurant manager but if you want something different try the street vendors."

"Is it safe to eat?"

"Absolutely," she answered and walked off.

"Ok, thanks," Sadie said under her breath with a short wave.

Sadie pushed her bike farther down the road to an area that was filled with smoke coming from homemade grills that lined the road. She read each sign as vendors verbally announced what they had and shoved samples in her face.

A tall thin man stepped in her path. "Ganga?" he asked with glazed eyes.

She held up her hand. "No thank you."

A lady grabbed her arm causing her to drop her bicycle. "You come here and try the lobster." Sadie was startled at first. "That guy won't hurt you but he won't leave you alone either." She smiled.

"Thank you." She looked over the lady's shoulder at the fifty-five gallon drum cut in half, grilling four lobsters. "That does look good."

"Sit here." The lady parked her bike for her and sat her in front of a rickety table. She placed a steaming lobster in front of her and Sadie cracked open the shell and bit into the meat allowing the savory flavor flood her mouth. *Wow*! she thought letting her eyes talk for her.

"It's good, right?"

"It's delicious." She took another bite, and before she realized it, she had inhaled the lobster. The lady took ten dollars from her and Sadie pushed her bike the rest of the way walking off what she had just eaten. People from different cultures and different countries staggered down the road as the wind from the ocean blew through cooling off the area. She heard three or maybe four different languages but even with lack of communication it was obvious that everyone was happy–including Sadie.

Barely having time to push her bike in the wobbly bike rack, she heard, "There's Atlanta." Finn leaned over the bar. "Where's the rest of the posse?"

"I think they're still getting ready."

"For what? This is island time. Wash your hair and throw on some clothes."

Sadie sat in one of the permanent bar stools that were buried in the sand. "So, what is this craft beer you were bragging on?"

The man she sat beside turned. "Honey, this is better than craft beer. This is a master brewer standing in front of you. I'm Gary by the way," he said loud enough for everyone to hear.

"Master brewer?" she said, exaggerating. Finn took down a Pilsner glass and twirled it in the palm of his hand. "I'm having deja vu of the movie Cocktail." She laughed.

"Bite your lip," Finn said looking at her. "Coughlin's law, never compare one bartender to another." He smiled.

"Who the hell is Coughlin?" B appeared behind the bar.

"You know the 80s movie called Cocktail." He handed Sadie the glass without letting go, "Have you ever drank, or did you quit for a reason?" He looked at her.

"I stopped last year, trying a healthier lifestyle." She pulled on the glass.

He raised one eyebrow. "A girl that quit beer for a healthier lifestyle . . . them be cursed words," he said in a pirate voice.

"So if I take a drink of this here lager I can break the curse." She playfully eyed him down.

"I would think so . . . but this is a Gose. A lime Gose to be precise." And with a dramatic wave, "I give you Finn's Summer Time."

The cold glass met the lips of Sadie and with a slight tilt the lightly foamed beer slowly went into her mouth, a smile formed. "This is really good."

Finn threw his towel over his shoulder and with a sarcastic grin, "I know. Stick with me, kid. I won't let you down."

twelve

The thoughts of a thermos crossed Sadie's mind as she peddled back to the resort with two cups of coffee spilling in her basket. The steam from her coffee drifted in the breeze as she got comfortable in a chair and stared out toward the reef that broke the waves on the horizon. She looked down at her phone and figured Paige was getting ready for work.

> *Good morning!*
> *Pictures?* Paige asked.
> *Of?*
> *The bartender!*
> *Oh*, she typed with her knees pulled to her chest sitting in an Adirondack chair. ***Turns out he owns a brewery here on the island and is from Brevard, NC.***
> *Is his beer sold here?*
> *No, just on the island . . . and I think just at his place.* She thought about it for a moment.

Wait! Am I talking with Sadie? The Sadie I know wouldn't know this much about a guy in just three days.

Oh, haha. She agreed with Paige; it was either something about being alone, hanging with the Texas girls, or the island, but she liked the new her.

Hearing footsteps on the dock and feeling it shake she turned, expecting to see one of the Texas girls. Instead she found RK walking toward her.

"Good morning," he said when she turned.

"Good morning."

"Probably the best place for coffee."

"Where's your cup?"

"I just put on a pot and saw you sitting out here." He leaned against the railing standing at a respectful distance. "You should take out one of the kayaks this morning."

"I'm not a very good boater person." *If that is even a word.*

"Today would be the best time, little wind and if you got tired or in trouble you could paddle to shore and ask for a ride back here. It's safe. On the other side of the island is a place where you can feed the Tarpon."

"I take it Tarpon are fish?" she asked.

"Yep, big silver fish. Then after the Tarpon you could stop and shake Finn and wake him up."

It took a second for the words to register. *Wake up Finn? Why in the world would I go into Finn's house and wake him?*

"I'm not sure how to respond to that!" Her tone changed.

RK laughed. "I didn't mean it like that. Finn lives on a boat. You could rock it to wake him up."

Ok, this Finn is getting more interesting by the moment. "I don't think I need to wake him," she said. "But I would like to take out a kayak." She pulled herself out of the chair.

Moments later, after packing a small bag of bottled water and sunscreen, Sadie and RK met on the beach beside a bright-yellow kayak. With instructions on how to paddle, he pushed her off into the clear blue waters of the island. "And Finn's boat is the first one you come to after the Tarpons. It has a blue hull and pirate flag on the bow," he yelled.

Managing the kayak was much easier than she expected and once she cleared the docks, she pulled out her sunscreen and lathered up for her first excursion. The entire trip around the island only took two hours and with a calm day and no head winds, she managed to get to the back side of the island with no problem.

The mangroves grew along the edge of the island hiding any beach or man-made structures giving her an isolated feeling. But when she spotted a couple of boats with kids feeding the Tarpons, that feeling left. Her kayak glided over the school of silver fish that broke the surface eating the food the young kids were throwing out. The smiles and laughter from the kids placed a smile on her face and watching them, she noticed a boat with a blue hull.

With her hand blocking the sunlight she watched the boat as Finn stepped out. *Why not*? She nodded to herself and paddled toward him.

He looked up and waved as Sadie was paddling toward him. "I see you are adapting to the island life." He put one foot up on the side of the boat.

"I see you don't get up with the sunrise," she said not realizing she was going faster than she expected. Trying to back-paddle, Sadie rammed the side of his boat with her kayak. She covered her mouth and her eyes widened twice their size.

"If you back up and paddle harder you might put a hole in it," he said leaning over, looking at where she hit his boat.

Embarrassed she said, "I am so sorry. I've never been in a kayak."

"Ah, don't worry. She's tough as nails and can take anything dished out to her." He patted the side of his boat.

"I think I left a mark." She pointed to a white mark on the blue hull.

"Give's it character. But I do expect compensation for the damage."

"Money?" She looked at him over her sunglasses.

"Breakfast." He leaned toward her and held out his hand to help her up on the boat. She reached out locking hands and, with one strong pull, she landed on the side of his boat. Standing above him in her two piece he placed both hands on her hips and lowered her into his boat. Her heart skipped three beats.

"I need my bag." She stood to the side and allowed Finn to reach down toward the small rope tied to the front of her kayak. The rope in one hand and his coffee in the other suddenly he lost his footing and went over headfirst. "Oh my gosh!" she screamed and rushed to the side of the boat.

Finn slowly surfaced with a smirk on his face. "Didn't expect that." Sadie looked down trying her hardest not to laugh but couldn't hold back,

"Yes I know, I'm so funny. Give me a hand." He reached up.

She grasped his hand. "I'm not strong enough to pull you . . ." Her words were interrupted with a strong tug pulling her over and into the water. Surfacing she was met by Finn laughing and, after a few splashes, they climbed out, tying the kayak to the dock.

"My bag," she said fetching it out of the water.

He handed her a towel. "Was something in there not waterproof?"

"Just my dry shirt."

He opened the door to the cabin and reached in pulling out a folded light blue Drifters Reef t-shirt. "This should fit."

She held it up. "My first island shirt." She took the towel he handed her, then pulled the shirt on.

"Looks good on you," he said drying off. In a low voice he added, "Everything looks good on you."

Butterflies filled her stomach. He probably hadn't meant for her to hear that, but warmth spread through her limbs.

"Right back atcha," she whispered.

thirteen

Sadie sat on the bow of Finn's boat with thoughts of him running through her head– along with her new feelings, Paige at home, and a host of other things. She felt the boat dip to her right and, looking back, saw Finn walking up to join her. "Sorry you fell in." She smiled.

"Hazards of living on an island."

"Do you go out much?" she asked realizing he might not know if she was talking about the boat or dating. "The boat."

"Nah, she's not running right now."

"She? What do you call her?"

"I haven't named her yet."

"Isn't that bad luck, not naming a boat?"

"Ah, just for superstitious people. You superstitious?" he asked.

"Maybe." She grinned.

The boat rocked back and forth causing their conversation to end. Finn glanced back.

"I thought I recognized that kayak," RK said joining them on the bow.

Sadie checked to make sure hers was still tied, her arms feeling heavy with the work out she earned paddling from the resort. *Or maybe it was the 5-minute water fight,* she thought. Either way, she questioned whether to continue her journey around the island, a question that was answered by RK. "Are you still kayaking or do you want me to haul it back?"

She started to answer when Finn interrupted her. "Haul it back. I'm going to get Atlanta to help me at the shed." At her expression he said, "I mean Sadie. Sorry, I'll stop calling you Atlanta."

"Thank you and what's the shed?"

"That's where I brew my beer and I am starting to can some today."

"And what makes you think I want to work on my vacation?"

RK laughed. "I'll let you two work this out. I'll stop by later and grab the kayak if it's still here.".

Sadie wasn't sure if Finn was confidant she would say yes to everything, or that he was just clueless when it came to girls. Something that she was interested in finding out. "I'll help, but it'll cost you." She nudged him.

"Deal. How about we start with a fresh fruit juice?" He pulled her to her feet.

"Maybe." She eyed him.

The island was now more alive than she'd found earlier with both tourist and locals walking to their destinations. The streets grew hot with the sun blazing down, and the wind from the ocean struggled to make it through the buildings. Finn handed her a ten-dollar bill. "Get me a watermelon, please." He nodded toward a small juice stand covered by old palm leaves.

"So now I'm your assistant?" She raised her brow.

"The shed is just around the corner and I want to straighten it up before you see it."

"Ok."

Met with a big smile from the lady behind the counter, Sadie scoured the menu as a young boy unloaded fresh fruit from his makeshift trailer attached to his bicycle. The aroma of pineapple, watermelon, and other fruits filled the area making it difficult for her to order. The lady looked past her. "Usual?" she asked someone behind Sadie.

"Yep."

Sadie recognized the voice and turned to find B standing behind her. "Good morning."

"Yep."

Looking for a conversation, "I really enjoy the food at the restaurant."

"I don't cook, just serve it." B reached around her for her juice and started to walk off, "How long are you here for?"

"A month," she answered, a little surprised, then stopped B with a follow up question, "Why?"

"You girls come and go. Normally Finn isn't the one to find interest in a tourist but for some reason he finds you interesting," she said with her left hand resting on her hip while holding her juice with the other.

The remark took Sadie by surprise, normally she would be all jittery learning that someone was interested in her but not in this way. Paralyzed, she tried to say something but found that B had turned her back and marched off. With B's words racing through her head and carrying Finn's watermelon juice, she stopped at the shed.

"Did you already drink yours?" Finn smiled leaning against the doorframe to the shed.

"No, I didn't feel like... here's your change. I don't feel all that well and I'm going to head back to the resort." She handed him a five dollar bill.

"I'm sorry, do you want me to get a golf cart to take you?"

"No, I'm ok. The walk with help me. I'll catch you later."

***

Finn stood in the doorway confused watching Sadie walk down the sandy road and disappear around the corner. He wasn't sure if it was something he had said or if she really didn't feel well. Setting his canning machine closer to the door to catch any breeze that happened to find its way through the buildings, he heard a voice come from outside. Glancing outside he saw B.

"What did you say to her." He quickly figured it out.

"Oh, don't get all huffy. You don't need to fall for some Georgia peach when she's going home in a few weeks."

"B, you're not my match maker or my mother."

"If it wasn't for me that crazy brit would still be around."

He took a deep breath saying, "Please stop. I am grateful for you helping me with my last girlfriend but they aren't all crazy."

"They're all evil."

"You're calling yourself evil." He chuckled.

"Damn right I am," she answered like it was applied.

Finn closed the doors to the shed and locked it eyeing down B. "You're going to apologize to her."

"Ha." She turned and left.

Finn jogged down a back road trying to catch up to Sadie with his flip flops dragging every step he took. A few locals yelled *hello* but his mind was in one place. Almost out of nowhere a six-seater golf cart cut around the street and swerved to miss him.

"Finn!" Four of the six Texans yelled from the cart.

"Ladies."

"Aw…. are you actually chasing Sadie?" one of them asked.

"Kinda… have you seen her?"

The girl driving pointed back with her thumb. "She's walking down the dock. Sure you want a

Georgia gal? There is nothing like a Texas girl!”
She devilishly grinned.

He laughed. “See y’all at the bar tonight.” He
jogged on.

fourteen

The aroma of fresh paint hit Finn before he could reach the resort, noticing the guard shack was changing colors. One of the workers from the resort balanced on a ladder holding a paint brush in one hand and holding the ladder with the other stretching out to reach an unpainted area. The slogan of the island, *Go Slow,* applied to everyone and there was no hurry to finish the guard shack in one day.

"Finn!" The worker brightened up seeing him walk up.

"Have you seen Sadie?"

"The girl from Georgia?"

"Yes."

He flicked paint as he pointed toward the dock with his brush. "There."

Sadie sat, looking confused, in one of the Adirondack chairs watching the waves break over the reef in the distance.

Finn walked to the dock slowly, rehearsing what he should say. "Don't pay B any attention."

"Oh, hey." She looked back.

Finn repeated the comment.

"Don't worry. It's good to have someone be protective."

"Well, she was out of line and had no business telling you… whatever she said."

"It's ok." She tried to play it off. Finn leaned on the railing looking out into the distance, thinking of what to say next as the wind blew through his hair. Sadie beat him with a question. "When someone is protective of another it usually means they were hurt. I don't mean to pry, but is that why you moved here?"

Finn turned with an uncomfortable grin. "No. When I moved here I started dating a girl who was a little crazy. Everyone saw it but me, and B stepped in and kinda saved me."

"Oh."

"You are just convinced that something tragic happened for me to move here." He laughed.

"No, I'm not." She took a deep breath before speaking. "It's just that a young guy like you up and moving to a small island is… a big move."

Then it hit Finn, something bigger than a vacation brought *her* here. "Ok." He sat in the chair beside her. "My father is a big tycoon in the beer industry and expected me to take over the business but wanted me to run it his way."

"If it works don't fix it." She repeated the words of her father.

"That's the problem. Sales were starting to decline and with the millenniums coming into drinking age they wanted something different. He isn't interested in any changes. One day we had a blow up and . . . three weeks later I found myself working at the place I own now."

"You bought the only bar on The Split?"

"No, there were three others when I bought it, but Mother Nature blew them away leaving half a building that I rebuilt, and Drifters Reef was born."

"So you are the drifter?" She giggled.

"Not really. This island is known for backpackers that travel the islands is search for a simple way of life. They just drift from place to place with no worries." He paused. "If it works don't fix it." He cut his eyes at her.

She smiled and for a long period they just sat quietly watching the ocean.

"And you call your beer Drifters Beer?" she asked nodded to a sign on his shed.

"Yep."

"What are you calling the lime beer I tried the other day?"

He shifted toward her. "I was thinking about . . . Lime." He laughed.

She shook her head and rolled her eyes. "No. You have to call it something." She tapped her fingernail against her teeth. "How about Horizons, with the drawing of a sunset on the can?"

"Horizons?" He sat back in his chair. "I like that." Then he bolted up and stuck his hand out to shake. "You're hired, and we can talk more about branding Drifters Beer tonight over supper."

Sadie's eyes widened. "Hired? Supper?"

"Deal." He shook her hand and jumped to his feet. "I'll swing by around 6 and pick you up."

"Like a…date?"

"Sure."

"I just had a not so pleasant conversation with B and now you are . . ."

"I'm not proposing, it's just supper. I know a perfect small place on the leeward side that has great ceviche. I have to go can beer this morning but I'll see you tonight." He jogged off before Sadie had a chance to change her mind or even answer.

***

What just happened? I went from stay away to a date. What's happening to you Sadie? You come to Belize and become nosy and a flirt. Looking back and not seeing anyone, she stripped down to her bikini and stepped off into the waters that flowed under the dock. A few strokes and she was in a sandy spot where her feet could touch. With a more few strokes, her feet left the sand and slowly floated to the surface allowing her hair to float in all directions. She drew in a few deep breathes. Snow white clouds floated by making it the perfect time and a chance for her to clear her head.

Just as she began to settle down and calm the butterflies in her stomach, a shadow appeared over her and continued forward until a large splash blinded her for a second. *Bird!?! Shark!?!*

"What the hell!" she screamed.

Finn surfaced in front of her. "Screw work today!"

96

"Ok?" No doubt her face showed her surprised.

"Who says a date has to be at night. We can start now."

"And who said I agreed to go on a date with you?"

"Oh?"

She could see the fear of rejection come over his face. "But since I don't have much to do today and since I don't know anyone on the island..." She grinned.

"Go slow."

Go slow? Is he telling me I'm coming on too fast? He is the one forcing a date on me. Then it hit her, the island slogan.

"Go slow." She smiled and joined hands with him. Their sudden touch sparked more than they expected and after a short awkward pause of staring at each other, six Texas girls barreled into the water around them.

"Don't know anyone?" He smiled.

"Well, almost," she answered as all six girls surfacing at the same time.

"I told you we were breaking up a moment," one of them said.

"They're still dressed. This isn't a moment is it?" another girl replied.

Finn laughed. "You're good. Plus Sadie and I are champions at chicken fighting. Unless you six think you can beat us."

He swam under Sadie's legs lifting her out of the water on his shoulders. The butterflies returned with his hands on her legs.

One of the girls followed suit and lifted an unexpected girl on her shoulders. "You're on, island boy!"

The fight broke out and as water splashed, Sadie laughed like she hadn't in a very long time.

fifteen

Two of the Texas girls lay across one of Sadie's beds looking at a vacation magazine. Sadie appeared from the bathroom in shorts and a light grey shirt. "Nope," one of the girls replied looking up.

Sadie took a deep aggravated breath and marched back to the bathroom shedding the clothes and dropping them in a pile. "I'm running out of clothes," she yelled through the door. *Why do I feel like Paige is here!*

"Whatcha got left?" One of the girls pushed her way into the bathroom. Sadie quickly backed out of the way covering her body with a towel. "You have got to lighten up. If you can't be naked in front of me how are you going to be undressed in front of Finn?"

The door swung open wider on the remark. "Oh my gosh. Are you planning on sleeping with him tonight?" the other girl asked.

"No!" Sadie blurted. "Read my lips, I am not sleeping with Finn tonight or any other night. I just met him."

"Uh huh, tell it to someone else," the first girl said.

"Wear this shirt." The other girl grabbed a shirt from the pile. "And those shorts." She pointed.

"Ok, ok. Let me get dressed." She pushed both of them out of the bathroom and got dressed. The mirror told the story of the night, a nervous girl who felt like it was her first date. She heard the girls laughing, and pushing the door open she saw them with her phone on the bed. "What are you doing?"

"Paige said she's proud of you and gives you a pass to sleep with Finn tonight."

"Paige? Give me the phone." She saw a complete conversation the girls were having with her friend in Atlanta. "You two are like little sisters."

She typed a message to Paige.

One of them hugged her with both arms. "I'm your sister. Just sucks we have to leave in two days and you'll be another three weeks. Can I stay with you?" She lit up.

"You have class." The other girl pushed her.

Before anyone could saying anything, a knock came from the door, all three girls looked at each other. "If it were the other girls they'd just walk in. What time is it?"

Sadie looked at her phone. "Six."

Both girls sat up with smiles. "It's him!" they said at the same time. Sadie rolled her eyes thinking she was back in middle school. "Give me your phone." One of them snatched it out of her hands. "I'm going to video this."

"Turn that off." Sadie tried to retrieve the phone but another knock pulled her to the door.

Flip flops, khaki shorts, and a white button up shirt, Finn stood at the door.

"Hey." The butterflies returned.

"You ready?" he slowly asked looking past her at the two girls videoing their conversation.

"Don't mind them." She waved him in and motioned for the girls to stop filming. They just laughed, now taking pictures of them.

"Get together for one pic."

Sadie started to say something but was pulled back to Finn's side with his arm around her "Awesome," one of the girls said while sending the picture to Paige. Sadie and Finn started a small conversation when the girl spoke back up. "Paige said he's freaking hot and not to come back to Atlanta."

"Give me that. . ." Sadie dove in for the phone wrestling it away from them as Finn laughed covering his red face. "We better go before they say something that will embarrass us both. Bye, girls." Sadie ushered Finn out the door.

"We love you, Sadie," she heard before her door closed.

"You have quite the friends," Finn said jogging down the stairs. A blue golf cart waited at the bottom of the stairs. "RK is loaning us his cart for tonight."

"Where is your cart?"

"I don't need one." He peeled out and turned sharply causing her to grab on, reminding her of riding with her older brother on the golf course. She spent many Sunday afternoons riding with her brother and watching him play a sport that he loved, learning it from their father.

A voice jerked her out of her thought. "You're being awfully quiet."

"Sorry, just thinking about family."

"Homesick?"

"Nope." She wanted to lean on him, grab his hand, and touch him some way, but she restrained herself and listened to him talk about a volleyball tournament he was hosting the following night. The golf cart slid to a stop. "This is a restaurant?"

"I didn't say we were going to a restaurant," he answered as Tekka opened the front door. "But I did promise you the best ceviche on the island." He hopped out.

"Finn is scared of dating and asked us to babysit. You want a beer?" RK appeared behind his wife.

"Really?" She grinned at Finn.

"No, I just want good food and . . ." He turned to RK. "What kind of beer?"

"Beer from the mainland, since you won't give me any of yours."

Tekka put her arm around Sadie. "This conversation is going to take longer than we're interested in hearing; help me in the kitchen." The girls disappeared inside while the guys loudly argued about beer and the reason RK invited them over was to occupy his wife.

Making sure each glass had the same amount of ice, Sadie watched out the open window at the boys standing on the back deck, and Finn who didn't seem aware of the staring eyes.

The sun in the backdrop shined across a calm ocean casting an orange glow on the horizon. "Sadie came up with the idea of putting that on my lime beer can," Finn pointed out.

"The ocean?"

"A sunset with the beer called Horizons."

"Cool," RK replied.

Tekka smiled. "It's been awhile since I have seen him happy," she said quietly.

"Really? I was told to stay away."

"Let me guess, B?"

"Yep."

"Don't pay her any attention. She's just being overprotective," she said walking outside with a large bowl of ceviche and a stack of four plates.

The evening turned into night with the two couples laughing at a story over drinks and food. *Wow, I came to vacation and spend time alone and here I am,* Sadie thought. *So much for doctor's orders to relax and remove any stress. Please God don't let Travis screw this up.*

sixteen

"Finn, we need to talk." B stormed down the steps into the bar.

"I know what you're going to say, and I really don't need any advice on dating right now. Plus, I have a bar and restaurant to run." Glasses clanked as he shoved them on a shelf.

B's hands went to her hip. "Who's running a restaurant?"

"You know what I mean."

"I do, and you can screw up your personal life if you want. This has to do with this two-bit bar hussy you hired to pour drinks. When you're not here, she has been stealing!"

Finn stopped what he was doing and gave B his attention. She was defiantly one to complain and give everyone hell, but she would never blame someone for doing something if it wasn't true–plus she treated his place like it was hers. "I'm listening."

"I came down last night, while you were off on your date," she said sarcastically. "And I stood right here and watched her pocket six drinks. Six drinks that didn't make it to the cash register."

"Well hell. I have noticed we are coming up short on nights I wasn't here."

"Let me guess. You thought it was because you weren't here," she replied with a smirk.

"Well of course." He laughed trying to change his mood, it didn't work.

Finn had asked Sadie to go on a paddle board trip in a mangrove island southwest of Caye Caulker but now that idea was shot out of the water. Now he had to fire someone. Stacking glasses, he let his thoughts wander from firing someone to last night with Sadie.

He faded off into a daydream. Once they had finished eating at RK's house, Finn drove her down an off-the-beaten path to a small sandy beach on the south end of the island. With water splashing around their ankles, they staggered through the sand talking about his family.

A half-moon lit the beach just enough to see where they were stepping and enough to see the stars in the heavens ripple in the reflection of the water. Unbeknownst to Sadie, who was pulling her hair out of her face and looking for seashells, Finn experienced butterflies like he'd never had before. Reaching for her hand with intentions to spin her around into his arms, three teenagers ran out onto the beach interrupting his attempt.

Still in his daydream, "Damn teenagers!" Finn said stacking glasses.

"What did teenagers do?" Gary's booming voice fill the small space as he plopped onto a bar stool.

"Oh hey, Gary." Finn shoved the last glass on the shelf. "Nothing, just thinking. Say, I have something to show you." He reached in his pocket and pulled out a crumbled piece of paper with a sunset drawn on it and the word *Horizons* written across it.

Gary examined the paper. "Failed art class, huh?"

"You get the gist of it."

"I like it. Good thinking about creating a brand for each beer."

"I'd like to take credit but it was Sadie's idea."

"Ah, the marketing girl from Atlanta. I just saw her. Down at the mini donut shop. Do you mind if I work on this?" He looked at Finn.

Finn ducked under the bar flap. "Pour yourself a beer, I'll be right back." He darted off.

***

"Hey B, is Finn around?" Sadie asked jogging up to the bar.

B was heading upstairs and took a couple of deep breaths before turning and facing Sadie.

Sadie swallowed hard at the expression on B's face. "Should I come back?"

Gary shook his head yes and B eyed her up and down. "I just had to fire someone a few minutes ago and now you come bee-bopping up–" B stopped. "Hey, you ever worked behind a bar?"

Sadie looked at Gary then back to B again. "No."

"You know how hard it is to put up with drunks, stay up all hours of the night, to clean puke from the bathroom, and then doing it all over again the next day?"

"No?"

B walked up to the bar and leaned over. "I don't know your angle or your interest in Finn and I don't know your story, but it seems his mind is elsewhere and if I am going to have to accept you. .

.” she threw a towel in the sink, “you’re going to have to earn my respect!”

Sadie thought for a moment that she wasn’t making any sense “I don’t know what you’re talking about.”

“I just fired a bartender because Fin’s been spending too much time with you. And . . . she was stealing while he was gone.”

“I’m sorry.”

“Don’t say you’re sorry. You’re hired, now get your ass over here and let me show you how to work the cash register.” She lifted the bar flap.

“Hired?”

“I would just go with it,” Gary suggested.

Straightening up and cocking her head, Sadie said, “Ok, you have a new bartender.”

A few instructions and an approved nod from B, and Sadie was pouring frosted beer glasses and laughing with Gary and a few others who had witnessed the fire and hire.

Out of breath and sweat dripping from his forehead Finn appeared beside Gary. “I couldn’t catch her, any idea where she was headed?”

Gary smiled and pointed across the bar, saying, “You mean our new bartender?”

Sadie turned and gave a small wave.

"Oh, hey. What are you doing back there?" He was still panting.

"Let her be at her new job and get up here so we can place an order from the distributor!" B ordered from the top of the stairs.

"New job?"

"I fired the hussy you hired and since you were spending your time with Miss Atlanta – well I hired her! Close your mouth, wipe the drool, and get up here."

Sadie felt the blush from B's words turn her face bright red.

Finn grinned and shook his head. "Ok, I can go with this." He looked at Gary. "You two get together and figure out what I am going to call my IPA."

"I hope you know what that is," Gary said to Sadie.

"Indian Pale Ale," she answered. She already had an idea for the label art.

Go Slow

seventeen

Sadie lay in bed ignoring the beam of sunlight landing on her bed. She wasn't sure what was heavier, her body or her eyes after a late-night at Drifters Reef. B was right, it wasn't easy work but with a promise from Finn to take her on a paddle board trip, it was worth it.

Water dripped from the air conditioner with condensation and even though sunlight made it through the window, the coldness of the room fogged the glass not allowing her to see out.

A knock pulled her out of falling back to sleep. *What do they want now*? She knew it was the Texas girls. She wrapped a sheet around her body and opened the door–not to the Texas girls but to Finn.

"Good morning!" He smiled holding a large coffee.

"What are you doing?" she asked though the sheet that was covering half her face.

"We are going paddle boarding this morning."

"It's too early."

He laughed. "Get dressed, I'll be in the office with RK." Without answering she shut the door then yanked it open and grabbed the coffee before closing it again.

A splash of cold water on her face didn't work but after a cool shower she was somewhat awake. She stumbled down the stairs and one of the Texas girls stopped her. "Today is our last day. We want you to hang out with us."

"I would love too…" Sadie started but the girl saw Finn standing in the doorway to the office.

The Texas girl smiled. "I see you have a date for today. Tonight, promise you'll hang out with us."

Sadie kissed two fingers and crossed her heart. "Promise."

"You ready?" Finn asked.

"I guess. I hope I don't fall asleep on you today," she replied then quickly thought that didn't sound the way she meant.

"Me too."

She laughed. "Not that you're boring, I just–"

"I know what you meant." He smiled.

A stop at the coffee shop for refills and two small bags of mini donuts helped Sadie wake up and start making sense. The mini donuts had become an addiction for her; she didn't have to chew they just melted in her mouth.

After the bag was devoured, they pulled up to the only surf shop on the island with a couple of locals stacking boards outside. "Aloha," one of them yelled at Finn.

"Morning." Finn shook his hand and gave him a one arm hug. "This is Sadie."

The short local gave him a smirk. "I figured that, you've been talking about her for a week." He shook Sadie's hand. "I'm Zac."

"I have. . . I mean, no I . . . don't say that. . ." Finn stumbled over everything he was trying to say.

A dark complected and muscular young woman walked up. "I like seeing him embarrassed. My name is Shar."

Sadie laughed at Finn's struggle. "Hi Shar, nice to meet both of you," she said.

"Zac here is a true descent of the Mayan tribe and a devoted member to restore their traditions," Finn replied.

She looked puzzled. "Mayan? I thought they disappeared a long time ago."

Zac laughed. "That was during prohibition, we're back now." He turned his attention to Finn and two paddle boards.

Shar picked up on her confusion. "There are different tribes still around. Come with me and I'll help you pick out a rash guard."

Browsing through the different color shirts, Sadie kept looking at Shar's cut body and muscles. "You are so fit," she said after Shar caught her eyes.

"I have four brothers who are into every sport you can think of." She smiled.

"My brother Travis is a golfer. Must be why I'm not fit." She laughed.

They walked out to the same center console boat that had taken Sadie out snorkeling. It rocked back and forth, tied to the dock in front of the surf shop. Sadie helped Shar carry the paddles and ice cooler while the guys tied two boards to the canopy. The day was quickly heating up and with a shove from Shar's flip flops, the boat pushed off with Zac behind the wheel.

"Where is his paddle board?"

"He's dropping up off. This color looks good on you." Finn tugged at the lime green rash guard that Shar had helped her pick out. She smiled from his comment then faced forward as Zac throttled down pushing the boat into a plain and racing toward The Split. The morning crew, made up of B and one other person, waved at them as they shot through The Split and poured out into open water.

Sadie curled up on the bow and watched the crystal blue water disappear under the hull of the boat. A light tap on her thigh pulled her attention to the four dolphins racing in the wake of the boat, one followed by a small baby. Zac pulled back on the throttle as one of the dolphins broke the surface followed by another trying to outdo the first one. Sadie watched the dolphins play in the water, her hand dragging the surface, unaware of Finn watched her, smiling.

When Zac pointed the boat to the south end of a mangrove island, Sadie held on to the side and walked under the canopy to the console. "How long have you lived on Caulker?" she asked Zac.

"Since I was a teenager."

"Are you really a Mayan?"

He laughed. "I am. I am from Punta Gorda, it's just south of here."

"I'm sorry I don't mean to sound stupid, I just don't know much about the Mayan people." She felt embarrassed.

"Don't feel stupid. That's Finn's job." He laughed. "There are four indigenous groups in Belize. They are the Creole, Garifuna, Mestizo, and the Mayan People."

"You're trying to restore the traditions?"

"Just trying to keep the western world from ruling and running us out."

"Running you out?"

"You are going to get him on his soap box," Finn butted in.

Zac laughed. "Yes, she is." He looked at Sadie. "Tourists have been coming down here for years and the more that come the more they bring of their traditions. Don't get me wrong, we love people and love the tourists and the money they bring. We just don't want to be pushed out on how we do things in our country."

"I don't think I follow."

"I'll explain when I come back to pick you up." He pointed to the island in front of them. "This is probably the coolest paddle board tour in the world."

They motored into a nature break in the mangrove island and with a blink of an eye the world changed from blue oceans to clear water, green canopies, and abundant wildlife.

eighteen

Various birds flew overhead casting shadows on the water with the sun hanging above them. Each bird made a different sound, making the canal a jungle sanctuary of music and a welcome that would send chills to anyone that had never visited a mangrove island. Sadie was in awe, and, glancing down in the crystal clear waters, she witnessed the sea life just as alive as the trees.

Finn and Zac pulled down their boards and flipped them into the water, temporally disrupting the wildlife.

"You guys are set," Zac said.

The water was surprisingly cooler than Sadie expected as her legs dipped around her board. Pushing off the boat she caught a glimpse of a shadow under her board and with closer examination she realized it was a shark. She jerked her legs out of the water and shot a concerned looked at Finn.

Laughing, he said, "It's just a nurse shark. There is nothing here that can hurt you."

She fully trusted Finn but kept her legs out of the water. Zac caught Sadie's attention and said, "Actually, we've only had three people eaten here this past year. It's a good year."

"Oh, ha ha," she replied.

"Catch." Zac threw her a mask with a snorkel hanging off the side. "You'll love seeing them from down under."

"Thank you." She placed the mask on the front of her board. "Zac? I know Creole is a native language to indigenous people, how do you say goodbye?"

Zac smiled with her desire to learn and held up the *hang loose* sign with his hand. "Later dude!" He quietly motored out and disappeared leaving them alone in this magical place.

"If you want you can take off that snorkel off the mask. It kinda gets in the way." He demonstrated with his.

Her board wobbled in the water as she reached for the mask and before falling in, she went to her knees and fixed her mask. Back on her feet they slowly paddled through the openings of the island and along tight passages with branches of the mangroves gracefully dipping into the water. Small fish of various colors hovered under the coverage curiously watching them paddle.

"Two fish amaze me." Finn looked back at Sadie.

"What's that?"

"The Bat Fish and the Queen Angel."

"I've heard of the Queen Angel but what's a Bat Fish."

Back paddling and stopping his board he gently slipped off into the water with his mask and searched the bottom for a moment. Surfacing he motioned for her to join him.

"I'm good," she answered.

"There is nothing in here that is going to hurt you," he repeated. "Come see this fish before he swims away."

Cautiously she eased into the refreshing water and swam over to Finn. Pointing to the bottom she saw a weird black fish that appeared to have wings. "Oh my gosh, it does look like a bat."

"Come look." He pulled her hand and swam closer to the edge where the branches entered the water. He tried to let go of her hand but her grip tightened with no intensions of letting go. Bright red and yellow coral sponges formed on the mangroves giving more life to the underwater world, a world that Sadie was quickly getting lost in.

"It's beautiful," she replied pulling her face out of the water.

"It's a nursery."

"Nursery?"

"It's where life starts and small fish grow into large fish. This is how the islands around here started. It's what Caye Caulker looked like at one time."

Wow!

Back on their boards they paddled through the maze of canals and, the farther they went, the tighter the canals became. On her knees, Sadie pulled her way through tight spots by grabbing branches and laid on her stomach a few times to duck under limbs. The ripples in the water grew as they reached the north end of the island, popping into open water.

With the wind in their backs they floated down the west side of the island giving them a break from paddling, as well as another opening Finn paddled into. Leaving the wind and paddling back into the calm clear water off the island, Finn slipped off his board. "Ok, this is what I love about this island."

Sadie slid back into the water that was deeper than before but just as clear. The mangroves seemed to reach out farther giving more canopy to the fish below. Submerging, she watched Finn swim down and into the canopy, disappearing among the life of their underwater world. Re-appearing he surfaced. "Can you hold your breath?"

"You're looking at the regional 200 meter champion." She grinned.

"Come on." He reached for her hand and gave an assuring smile. His touch created a spark that Sadie couldn't explain and, pulling her down under the mangroves, she witnessed the beauty up close and personal. Then, like in a movie, a fish swam out and paused in front of them, its color something she had never seen before. The green, yellow, and neon blue didn't seem to have a starting or finishing point and from the graceful pose it had Sadie knew it had to be the Queen Angel fish he was talking about.

And as if giving Sadie her approval of Finn the Queen Angel slowly swam off. "Wow."

"That's my favorite."

The longer they explored the new world the longer it seemed Sadie could hold her breath until one of their last dives she watched Finn swim out ahead of her then came back. He grabbed her ankle

Lee DuCote

and walked his hands slowly up her body. His face came to hers and before running out of breath they locked lips and embraced under the surface.

Their bodies slowly floated to the surface never unlocking and she wrapped her legs around him sending chills up her spine. He carefully removed her mask and returned to her lips. Her heart skipped several beats when his hand ran from her side to her hip. In one motion he lifted her out of the water and onto her board. Carefully and with balance he crawled on the board. Sadie was on her back and Finn laid on top of her, running the back of his fingers on the side of her face; a touch that was indescribable to her.

A loud and piercing sound echoed through the canals. "Finn!"

Finn opened his eyes and looked at Sadie. "Damn Zac. He's been here a million times and still gets lost."

"I could stay here forever."

"It is beautiful."

"I was talking about this." Her expression didn't change.

He smiled. "So was I."

The hull of the boat rounded the corner with a wave from Zac greeting the couple that were swimming beside their boards. "How did you like the island?"

"I don't want to leave, it's incredible," Sadie answered as he pulled her out of the water.

"You need a hand?" Zac leaned over to Finn.

"Give me a moment." Finn waved him to get Sadie's board first.

She leaned over with a giggle. "Are you peeing?"

"Nope, I'm not European, I'm American." He laughed and swam to the back of the boat to climb in.

nineteen

Wrapped in both a towel and Finn's arms, Sadie remained in awe of her trip and the ending that could only be made in movies or books. Subtle smiles from Finn and his tight grip gave her the feeling that this wasn't a onetime thing.

Zac butted the hull of the boat on the dock that allowed boats to visit The Split, pulling her out of her pleasant haze of daydreams.

"Front door service," Finn said pulling Sadie out of the boat. Waving to Zac they walked to Drifters Reef with Finn's arm around her.

"Well hell! There goes the bar," B said with her hands on her hip.

"I am going to duck into your office and change," Sadie said ignoring B's comment. Finn held her hand, stretching out their arms making her spin and face him before she ducked into his office.

"This is going to be one of those sick cushy things, huh?" B eyed down Finn.

"You want details?"

Sadie could hear them from the office.

"Just give me the first opportunity at this place when you're forced to sell." B disappeared up the stairs but not before the "*woos*" of the Texas girls sounded as they pulled up in their golf cart. "And the hits just keep on coming." B continued up the stairs.

"Where's Sadie?"

"Changing in the office. She'll be right out. Whatcha starting out with?" Finn said.

"Something that has a kick," one of them replied.

"Wait, what was that 1980's drink that tasted like Dr. Pepper?" Another asked.

Finn lined six shot glasses on the bar. "Flaming Dr. Peppers," he said. "You guys watch one another tonight, this is strong."

"We will," she assured him.

The sounds of girls screaming and laughing drifted in the door to Finn's office where Sadie was being a little nosy as she looked at the pictures that lined the walls. Pictures of Finn when he was in high school to scenes of a man who had to be his father standing in front of vats in a brewery. She took down one of the photos of his family on the beach revealing an older looking sister and a happy mother with the words *Merry Christmas* posted on the bottom.

"Sadie?" a petite voice said as the door opened.

"Yes." She ducked into view.

One of the Texas girls stepped in. "Finn said you were in here changing." She paused looking at her "You're glowing! What happened today?"

How in the world can you tell? "We just went paddle boarding."

"And?"

Blushing and feeling like she got caught, she said, "We kissed."

"It must have been one hell of a kiss."

"Is it that obvious?"

"Only in a good way. Come have a beer with us." She pulled her out of the office, the picture left on his desk.

Sadie's name echoed through the bar from the Texas girls followed by a few *woos* that had B scowling as she served her customers. Sadie stayed behind the bar to help Finn pour drinks. "Are you working here too?" one of the Texas girls asked.

"Too? What other thing are you asking?" Finn raised an eyebrow.

"Just that she's in love."

A frosted mug slid in front of the girl. "Drink," Sadie said quickly trying to defuse where the conversation was going.

Finn just laughed and helped someone else.

The evening shift started with the girls leaning over the bar quizzing Sadie about everything like a bunch of middle school girls. She lost their attention when a boat full of dark-complected surfers landed on the dock. Finding her place behind the bar and practically rubbing elbows with Finn came easier than she ever thought. Watching him wait on customers… *What is it about this island? I have felt more at home in the last week here than all my time in Atlanta,* she thought.

After a busy night and at the sound of the bell symbolizing last call, Sadie noticed half the Texas girls asleep on a table near the dock; the other half still flirting with the surfers. Once the guys' boat pulled away from the dock leaving the girls, they staggered back to the bar.

"By the looks of things, I better drive them back to the resort," Sadie said to Finn.

"I was hoping we could have some time…"

"What about tomorrow?"

"I promised RK I would help him set out lobster traps for the lobster festival this weekend. You want to go with us?"

"Sure."

"We'll leave at 7."

"AM?" Her voice climbed an octave.

"Early bird gets the worm."

"I don't see how you do it. But ok, I'll go. Just don't expect me to stay awake the whole time." She wiped off the bar, then standing on her tip toes, she pecked his lips.

"You can do better than that." He tried to stop her.

With a seductive smile she said, "Gives you something to look forward to."

Two arms, three legs, and one head hung off the golf cart as Sadie drove the Texas girls back to the resort. She was happy they stayed at the bar all night where she could keep an eye on them. It was tougher getting them up to their rooms than it was to load them in the cart, but once everyone was safe inside, Sadie made it to her room.

Her phone buzzed with a text. ***How was today?*** Paige asked.

128

Heaven! she replied. Seconds later her phone rang with a call on Facetime. "You are going to run my bill up." Sadie greeted her face to face.

"If you're connected to internet it doesn't cost anything. Now spill!"

"He took me paddle boarding through a mangrove island today. It was so beautiful that I was . . ."

"Yah, yah and blah blah. Did you kiss him?" she interrupted. Sadie's smile and her red face answered the question. "Oh my gosh." Paige sat up. "Tell me everything!"

"I want to tell you about the island and the Angel Fish."

"I don't care about the island and a stupid fish. What happened?"

Sadie took a deep breath. "We were underwater looking at coral and fish when he swam up to me and kissed me underwater. Then, and I don't know how, he lifted me onto my board and climbed on top of me." She giggled.

"With or without your bathing suit?"

"With!" Sadie smirked.

"Of course. So… do you like him?"

"Is that possible after just a few days?"

"Yes. You're not being cheap."

"You read my mind. I miss you." A single tear formed in Sadie's eye. "I'm kinda scared."

"Being there by yourself? We talked about this a million times."

"I'm scared because I'm so comfortable here and it feels natural with him."

"You only live once. Right? Don't regret anything. Right?" Paige reminded her of their conversation.

"Right." The tear mingled with other tears falling onto her lap.

The girls talked for a few more minutes, then Sadie took a quick shower.

Tossing in her sleep Sadie found herself in a bizarre dream that started with her and Finn underwater and under the mangrove branches. He disappeared and re-appeared as the Queen Angel fish swimming around her desperately trying to gain her attention. She realized she was sinking into a deeper place without any breath or life. Sadie sat up in a sweat.

twenty

After spilling coffee every morning on the bike ride back to the resort, Sadie had picked up a thermos from the store. *An ingenious idea* was the remark from Lorene who filled her coffee every morning and someone who was slowly becoming a friend. Sadie had also become a fixture in the morning rituals sitting on the end of the dock waving to the man who paddled his boat toward the break and saying "good morning" to the three ladies that walked past heading to their cleaning jobs and receiving a blast from the water taxi that was always on schedule.

This morning was no different, with the exception of the water taxi. It was running late and for good reason; six Texan girls. Looking through the steam that rose from her cup she spotted the light green and yellow water taxi breaking through the blue water and headed toward Belize City. But this morning it seemed to be coming closer to the dock than normal and once it was near she realized why. Five loud horn blasts and five Texas girls waved goodbye, with the sixth girl hanging over the side throwing up.

With a giant wave back, she thought, *I am going to miss those crazy girls*. She could swear that two of them mooned her. As the green and yellow blended in with the horizon, a pair of hands ran along Sadie's side causing her to drop her coffee in the water "Holy . . ." She bit her tongue.

Laughing, he said, "I'm sorry." Finn replied looking over at her floating cup. "You shouldn't litter, we work hard at keeping Caulker clean."

"Jerk! You're going to have to get that." She punched him in the chest. Still laughing Finn dropped to his stomach and reached in retrieving the cup, then rolled over and reached up to Sadie wanting help to his feet. She pulled on his arm with smirk.

Suddenly white spots appeared in her vision and the water started spinning; she lost her strength and fell on top of Finn. No doubt thinking she was purposely falling in his lap he wrapped his arm around her and started to kiss her. "Sadie? Sadie?" He gently laid her to her side and climbed to his knees. "Sadie?" His voice grew. Frantic when she didn't answer.

Her eyes blinked several times trying to block the sun. "I'm ok," she said burying her head in her hands.

"You're scaring me. Are you sure?"

"Yes, I just got lightheaded. Let me sit for a moment. I think I got too much sun yesterday."

"But we were under the mangroves most of the day…" Finn said.

"Would you get me some water?"

"Absolutely." He dashed down the dock and ran to the office.

Sadie slid her fingers over her wrist and felt her racing pulse. *Deep breaths.* She repeated it over and over in her mind. The sound of Finn running back pulled her fingers off her wrist.

"Here." The cool water trickling down her throat felt good and gave her some relief. "Maybe you should stay here."

"Nah, I'll be ok. It will do me some good to be out on the water with a steady breeze." She started to her feet and smiled at him. "I'm sorry. Late nights, sun, and probably not drinking enough of water."

133

"Well, actually. I am hiring a new person today to help at the bar."

"I'm fired?" She tried to give him puppy dog eyes though they were probably red from rubbing them.

"No, promoted. You are now the marketing director of Drifters Beer."

"That sounds like a lot of work. Pouring drinks is a lot easier."

"Maybe, but the marketing director gets to spend her time with upper management," he flirted.

"I get to spend more time with B?" she smiled.

"Something like that." Finn spotted RK in the distance flying their way and pointed. "Here comes our ride. You sure you're ok?"

"Yes. Let me grab my bag and more waters and I'll be right back." With the beach still spinning she tried her best to hide the disorientation and walk back to her room.

After splashing cold water over her face, she changed into shorts and a tank top, then headed back to the dock. The boat that had taken her and the Texans out snorkeling, was covered with wooden traps and very little place to stand. "You sure you have room?"

"Of course. Plus, once we get to our spot these traps will be thrown over." RK helped her on the boat. Not only did the traps hinder the wind from cooling them down but had an indescribable smell from last year's season. But just as RK said, they reached their spot and one by one the traps left the bow until she could see over the others. RK moved their ice chest close to her. "Here's a place to sit."

"Thanks." She sat and cleaned the salt off her sunglasses. Finn and RK got back to baiting and setting traps leaving her to drift with her thoughts–thoughts that surprised her. She remembered spending a summer vacation with her parents on an island a few hours from Atlanta called Tybee Island.

Visions of a middle school kid hanging her head out the window, watching the city of Savannah come and go as they headed out to the marsh and the popular tourist spot. The first impact the small quaint island had on her was the lack of fast food chains and outdated buildings. But the beach was sandy and the water warm, giving her lots of room for castles and water fights with her father.

A man that had worked hard his entire life generating enough of money to send his kids to college and enough for a summer vacation that changed from year to year. Her purpose for starting a water fight with him was the moment he would lunge for her and with his callus hands lift her above the water and spin her in circles, followed by catching him in her arms. The smiles from his face never left her thoughts and the strength of his hands could still be felt on her arms; two things she prayed nightly she would never lose. Her mother would sit under the umbrella with an oversize straw hat and oversized sunglasses reading a different book every day. Sadie admired how fast her mother could read and remembered everything about the book for years, something her brother had inherited from her.

"Sadie?" Finn woke her from her thoughts.

"Yea?"

"You ok?"

She smiled at his persistence. "I am."

"Ok, could I have a water?" he asked.

"Oh, yes. Sorry, you caught me in thought." She got off the cooler she was sitting on and grabbed two bottles of water.

"It must have been a good thought. You were staring out into nothing."

"It was," she answered.

twenty one

Finn constantly threw baited traps into the water without his shirt on, keeping Sadie focused on their work and engaged in their conversation. RK swung the boat toward the reef staying just far enough away for the waves to have little effect on their course. He waved Sadie to the wheel. "See the needle pointing to 170." He pointed to the digital compass.

"Yes."

"Keep it on that course."

Finn stepped behind the center console with her and pulled out his phone and tuned into Spotify and connected to the radio. "And if you don't mind make sure we have tunes." He rejoined RK.

After half a chorus of a hip hop song she didn't recognize she changed his station to a Caribbean country station with the Zac Brown Band. "That's what I'm talking about," RK yelled over the music while Finn shook his head.

They worked for the remaining few hours of morning and finished just as the sun topped out over the small island. The boys washed their hands over the side of the boat then RK tried to relieve Sadie from the wheel.

"Um, no," she said, standing her ground. "I've already been fired today from bartending; you're not going to take my captain job. Have a seat boys." She throttled the twin engines and spun the boat around aiming at Caye Caulker.

"You got a tough one here," RK yelled at Finn.

"We'll see how tough she is tomorrow at the festival.-Lobster Fest in the biggest festival and lasts three days. Tomorrow is the big concert that kicks off the weekend."

Sadie giggled at the remark of Finn's screwed up mind. "Who's playing?"

"That's the cool part," Finn replied. "The island surprises everyone with a different band each year. No one knows until they get on stage."

"Sounds like fun." She held onto the wheel as they skipped across the waves and the clear blue water. The wind pressed against their sunburned faces and the nature smell of the ocean had returned with all the traps happily soaking on the sandy bottom of the Caribbean. RK slowly slipped behind the wheel pushing Sadie onto the ice chest with Finn. The weather was warm but feeling Finn's arm resting on her shoulder sent chills up her back and brought out goose bumps. She tried covering her arms hoping he wouldn't see.

The bow of the boat just touched the dock at Anchor Resort and Finn jumped onto the wooden planks catching a line from RK to tie up. After everything was situated, RK thanked them then jogged to the office to check in with his wife.

"I better head to my place and shower before heading to the bar," Finn said.

"You can shower here." She pointed to her room before she realized what she had offered. She stood nervously waiting for his answer.

Finn cocked his head. "You don't mind?"

"Nah." Her hands shook but she tried to play off her nerves.

"OK." He followed her to her room.

She fumbled with the keys unlocking the door and opened it to the cold room.

Finn entered like he'd been there a thousand times. "I'll just be a minute." He disappeared into her bathroom. She told herself she wasn't expecting anything by inviting him up. The door swung back open. "You need in here before I climb in the shower?"

"No!" Her voice shot up three octaves. "I'm ok," she said in a softer tone.

He laughed and closed the door. She started pacing the floor then looked in a mirror above the desk saying, "What am I worried about? Stop acting like a virgin on prom night." She nodded at herself then sat on the edge of the bed. She picked up a magazine the Texas girls had been looking at and flipped through the pages, trying to occupy her time.

Why would it be so bad if I climbed in the shower with him? If I were Paige, I would already be in there. No one would ever know, stop being so. . . so you! She stood up then sat back down. *That's not you; you don't sleep with someone you just met last week.* She fought with herself long enough for Finn to finish his shower.

"I probably could . . ." Finn said opening the door and witnessing Sadie throw the magazine to the ceiling and spring up from the bed. "You ok?" he asked drying his hair with a towel as he got dressed.

"Yes!" Her voice was still four octaves high. She cleared her throat. "I'm fine. You?" *Why did I ask that? You can be such a middle school girl!*

"Am I making you nervous?"

She shifted her weight twice and moved her hand three times from hip to hip. "No, why?"

"Never mind." He laughed, then said, "I was saying that I could use your help tomorrow at the bar before the concert, then we could go together."

"You don't need to stay at the bar or restaurant?"

"Nah, everyone goes to the concert. A lot of people come here tomorrow; it gets crowded but it's a lot of fun."

"Of course I can help."

"I kinda feel bad about asking when you're supposed to be on your vacation."

She shook her head. "Don't. I enjoy helping and . . . being with you." She took a deep breath.

He wrapped his arms around her waist. "I enjoy being around you too." He leaned down and kissed her, as they stared into each other's eyes without a smile or a hint of expression. Sadie wasn't sure if it was her heart beat she was feeling or his as their chests pressed against each other. She stretched up and kissed him again. This time his hand reached behind her head and they locked lips. Within a few seconds she back peddled toward the bed with him leading the way and together they fell across the bed, making out like a couple of high school kids.

Pulling back and looking down at her he said, "I'd like to stay all evening and maybe longer, but I have to start training my new person."

"I hope she doesn't steal too much of your time."

"She?" He thought a moment. "Her name is Benny and he is a local."

"Oh, I figured you'd hire a hot girl. You know for business." She laughed.

"People come to Drifters Reef for beer and food. And this hottie." He pointed to himself.

She pushed him and laughed. "You are so full of yourself."

"You coming by this evening?"

"Make time for me?"

"Sunset." He kissed her and dashed out the door leaving her on the bed with a racing heart and crazy emotions.

"Damn, I am falling in love!" She rolled over to text Paige.

twenty two

After a busy night training his new bartender, keeping up with a growing crowd for the festival, and handling B's complaints on not ordering enough fish, Finn called it an early night and dropped off Sadie at the resort. It was definitely a good call because Sadie didn't remember her head hitting the pillow before she was out. Even when she woke, the hum of the AC quickly put her back to sleep, a sleep that was much needed.

The warmth that massaged her face from one of the sun's rays pulled her out of a deep sleep and pleasant dream of her and her father. But the door slamming next door opened her eyes and woke her up. *Is it 9 o'clock*? She opened the door to the balcony and allowed the salty warm air inside.

The wind blew like it did every morning. The guys who worked at the resort were still painting the guard shack. "Good morning!" RK yelled from the front steps of the office. Sadie wrapped her arms over her t-shirt and waved back.

"Coffee!" he yelled pointing to the office. She gave another wave and, after changing, she skipped down the stairs and made her way to the office, flipping her hair in the wind.

"Thank you. I was wondering what I was going to do about my morning addiction." She greeted RK and Tekka who were glued to the computer screen.

"Are you going to the concert?" she asked Sadie.

"I think so. Do *you* know who's playing?"

"That's what I'm trying to figure out. They are tight-lipped about it around here."

"That's what Finn said." Sadie took a sip of her coffee. "Thanks," she said.

Tekka looked up to Sadie and said, "Are you feeling ok? You look pale."

Sadie yawned and said, "Just woke up." She poured another cup and stepped back out into the sun and headed to her room. She glanced in the direction of the two rooms the Texas girls stayed in and wondered how they were doing and what havoc they were causing.

She caught her cell phone ringing with a FaceTime message and opened it. "Good morning," she said to Paige.

"I'm not interrupting anything am I?" Paige greeted her back.

"I'm not you," she answered with a slur of sarcasm. "Why aren't you at work?"

"You sure have embraced the island life, it's Saturday."

"Oh wow, I guess it is." A knock came to her door. "Hang on." She dropped the phone on her bed. "Good morning," she greeted Finn.

"Indeed it is and I need help," he said.

"What's up?"

"I need help canning beer for tonight. . ."

"Is that him?" Paige's voice shouted from the phone.

Finn looked around Sadie, saying, "Who's on the phone" But he didn't give her an opportunity to answer, pushing around her to the bed, and picking up the phone said, "You must be the infamous Paige."

"And you are hot!" she answered causing him to laugh and look at Sadie.

Sadie shut the door and walked behind Finn so Paige could see her. "If you two are going to talk, try not to embarrass me." She closed the bathroom door listening carefully to their conversation and brushing her teeth at the same time. Before she could get out, Finn met her at the door. "Is she still on the phone?"

"Had to go." He took her by surprise and wrapped his arms around her, she blushed. "Do you mind helping me?"

"No." She returned the gesture of arms but beat him to the kiss.

***

With a cup in each hand, she balanced in RK's golf cart as Finn sped down the sandy roads toward the shed. Passing the coffee shop, Sadie held up a cup and yelled good morning to Lorene. Her face remained expressionless as she said nothing in return.

"What are you doing?" Finn asked.

"Just saying good morning. I guess I offended her holding up a coffee I didn't buy from her. I'll go apologize later."

"You need to stay away from Lorene."

"You know her? I mean, I guess you would, small island."

"You don't . . ." Finn started as a tourist on a bike turned into their path causing him to slam on his breaks and send Sadie toward the dash, losing one of her coffees. "Damn! Come on, guy, you got to watch out on the roads," Finn said losing his cool.

"Slow down," the man replied.

"Watch where you're going! We don't have a hospital."

"But we do have cemeteries." Sadie smiled hoping to ease the tension. The man said something, waved his arm in the air, and continued on his way. "Well, at least I have one cup."

They made it two more blocks and came to a squelching stop in front of the shed. Sadie sat in the cart finishing her coffee then joined Finn who had already unlocked the door and made it inside. "You seem to drive RK's cart more than he does."

"I normally never go to his resort."

"Oh."

"Ok, here's what I need you to do." He pulled her around to a stack of silver beer cans and showed her how to place them on a small conveyer belt that guided them into a machine that poured and sealed them. Not saying anything, she focused on placing the right amount of cans on the belt and fed the machine while Finn placed them in six packs and re-stacked on the other side.

"Are you ok? You seem miffed." She broke the silence.

"Yeah, just got to get this done for tonight."

She thought of something to talk about since he wasn't saying much. "I read an article on Ambergris Caye. I was thinking of going to see it."

"It's too busy for me," he said without looking up.

"Oh."

He stopped what he was doing and looked up. "I'm sorry. That sounded wrong. It is a busy island but if you want to go, I can take you."

"I want to see the secret beach."

He laughed leaving her to question her comment. "I'll take you. But first, the concert tonight."

twenty three

Sadie was astonished at the mass transformation of The Split that was now an anchor point for all types of boats and visitors that were gathering for the concert. A few multimillion dollar yachts with full crews pulled up, unloading people into smaller boats.

Sadie peeked at Finn through the corner of her eye and shook her head dumbfounded at the crowd. "Are we going to get a good seat?" she yelled over the noise.

"Seat? It's just a standing type concert. And yes, I've got us hooked up."

"You fix up that boat of yours and it might turn out something like that." She pointed to a snow-white yacht with neon blue lights shining down in the water.

"I'd have to bury what I have and hope it grows into something like that."

RK appeared and leaped over the bar like he owned the place. "Is it my shift yet?"

"About damn time you showed up," Finn said. "Sadie, could you help B? She is drowning with people upstairs."

"Of course." She smiled and jogged up the stairs.

"Where do you need me?" She ran into B.

"Those five tables," she replied balancing a tray of food and drinks.

"What number are they?" she asked having waited on tables in her college days.

"What the hell does it matter?" B scowled.

Sadie refilled waters, tea, and a dozen beers before taking their orders and like an old pro, placed the tickets in front of the cook. "Hold the onions on this one." She pointed to a ticket where she had drawn a line through the letter O, then returned to her tables.

"This one is a keeper," the cook said to B, smiling approvement at Sadie.

"Yea, she's starting to wear on me too."

That made Sadie happier than she would have thought.

A loud rumble filtered through the sandy roads and onto The Split, alerting everyone that

150

something was going on at the stage. The excitement of the sound drew a third of the customers who thought the concert was starting. Sadie ran down the stairs and looked at Finn. "Sound check, still got an hour," he said obviously reading her mind.

The hour passed in record time and soon Finn ran out of beer and food. The last customer upstairs paid his bill and scurried off down the road toward the concert.

Sadie finished cleaning off her tables. "You need me for anything else?" she asked B.

B placed both her hands on Sadie's shoulders and looked into her piercing green eyes. "Don't break his heart."

With a serious expression she said, "I promise B."

"You did good tonight, kid. Might have to keep you around."

"Thank you. Are you going to the concert?"

B laughed and took her tray into the kitchen, letting Sadie know that she wasn't going to the concert.

She wasn't sure why she was so excited about the concert, but she felt like a child on Christmas morning. Storming down the stairs she saw Finn throw his towel on the bar. "You ready?"

Locking fingers, they held hands as the concert started cranking up in the distance. The crowd bled into the streets and onto building roofs as a local band played first.

Finn pulled Sadie through part of the crowd and stopped at a door and walked in. "Whose place?" she asked.

"A friend with the best seat in the house." He pulled her up three flights of stairs and out onto the roof that was adjacent to the stage. A few people on the roof greeted them; no-one she recognized, then she peered over the side at the massive crowd below and the stage that lit up the area.

After a few reggae songs the local band left the stage and the mayor of the island walked out. "Welcome to Caye Caulker," he started. "It is my pleasure and great honor to introduce . . . Kenny Chesney and Ziggy Marley!" His voice echoed throughout the island followed by an uproar of people.

Sadie looked up at Finn who was standing behind her with his arms wrapped around her. "Are you freaking kidding me?" And before he could answer both Kenny and Ziggy walked out on the stage and instantly broke out into a Bob Marley song. For the next hour and a half they swayed to the Caribbean music of two legends who entertained the crowd.

Once the concert was over Finn pulled Sadie back down the stairs and out the back door.

"Where are we going now?"

"I want to beat the crowd and get to my boat."

"Ok? So, we are going to your place?"

"It's not like that. It's a sight to see all those boats race back to the mainland."

They jogged through the roads, around others who left early, like a couple of high school kids going to make out. Once at his boat, she pulled up short. "I think with some soap and water she could shine like those yachts."

"Trust me, it's going to take more than soap and water."

The rest of their evening was spent watching a mass exodus of boats leave Caye Caulker and disappear into the night toward the mainland. Finishing a red solo cup of Finn's Lime Gose, Sadie stood thinking it was the end of their night, but Finn cut her thought short by pulling her to him. She started to say something but his lips landing on hers cut all words she was going to speak. The warmth of his lips, the warmth of his arms, and the warmth of his hands that rested on her back turned knots inside her and sent her into a state where she had never been.

The sky was lit by the Caribbean stars and the west wind wrapped around the island sending a warm breeze across the deck of Finn's boat. Sadie struggled with the thought of staying the night and was conflicted on what to say to Finn. But being a southern gentleman Finn spoke up first, "My mind wants you to stay but my heart says we have time. Would it be ok if I drove you home?"

Sadie smiled. "Of course." Then the thought passed through her mind, *time*?

The night stayed passionate and romantic with the clouds crossing the moon while riding back to her room. She held Finn's left arm and gazed up at the stars with the thoughts of a perfect night.

You only live once.

Go Slow

twenty four

The following day started out with Sadie's normal ritual; going after coffee and drinking at the end of the pier. She sat in amazement and in awe with thoughts of last night playing over and over in her mind. The deep thoughts of Finn caused her to miss parts of her morning, like the man in the rowboat, the ladies walking to work, and the setup to paint the small guard shack. A brown pelican glided above the water in search for breakfast and in the background was the AM water taxi heading to Belize City.

What if I wake him up? She sprung up with her mind already made up. Peddling around locals and tourists, she waved at a group of men working on a house and then to a little girl dressed in her school uniform. *Why do I feel like I am a character out of The Sound of Music?* Turning on the road that led to Finn's boat she caught the glimpse of another bike parked on the dock beside his boat.

Pulling up she saw Lorene on the back of the boat with Finn. First thought was she delivered him coffee but then she realized his mood had changed yesterday after they saw her. She studied their body language, being too far to hear their conversation. *What am I missing*? She watched Lorene approach him and try to put her arms around. Sadie breathed a sigh of relief when Finn pushed her away.

Lorene climbed off the boat and aimed her bike in Sadie's direction. Sadie quickly pushed her bike behind a house and watched her pass unnoticed. She walked her bike up to the dock catching Finn by surprise. "I take it you saw that," he said.

"I did. What is that all about?" She held onto the handlebars.

He scratched his eyebrow then pointed in the direction of Lorene. "Meet the crazy ex." Sadie remained silent unsure what to say. Finn saw her expression. "Please trust me when I say ex."

"How long?"

"A year."

"How crazy?"

"I suggest you find another coffee shop." He stepped onto the dock. "Believe me, I have zero feelings. It's crap like this that makes me dislike her even more." Sadie looked toward the ocean in thought. "I think we are entitled to one crazy relationship, right?"

Yep, she thought. "I guess. Do I need to .. .?"

"No." He cut her off. "Don't let her ruin what we have." He placed his hand on top of hers and the warmth she felt last night returned.

She bit her bottom lip and nodded. "Ok."

"Thank you. Now, let's stop by the bar before we head out."

"Head out?"

"Ambergris Caye. You said you wanted to go."

"I did. Let me go gather a few things and I can meet you at the bar."

"We're taking RK's boat, so I'll meet you at the resort."

"It's nice to have friends with things." She grinned.

"Yep."

She rode back on a different route fearing Lorene would stop her. Finn didn't give her much time to get ready and pulled in the resort behind her. Within a short time she walked down the dock with a bag hanging on her shoulder and took Finn's hand to board the boat that was rocking back and forth.

The engines fired up pushing a puff of smoke across the water and into the wind. Sadie placed her bag under a seat and stood by the center console while Finn untied them. Clearing the pier, she switched to the cushion seat in front of the console and took a few deep breaths as the bow broke across the choppy sea. Nonchalantly glancing back, she watched Finn steer them toward Ambergris with his hat turned backward and the wind pushing his t-shirt tightly against his abs; she took another deep breath.

"I give you Ambergris Caye," he yelled above the engines as they hurled past resort after resort and the white sandy beaches. Sadie watched the island and noticed the traffic on the road between each building. They docked at a popular dive shop and after tipping the young local to watch the boat, they made their way to the town square. With just enough space to walk beside the road she was surprised at the grid-lock of golf carts and trucks. The smoke from a few tractor trailer trucks choked them out and sped up their walk.

"This is crazy."

"I told you it was busy."

"I didn't expect this. This is something like on TV, how do you get around?"

158

"You'll see. We have to rent a cart to get around and to the secret beach." He stopped at a street side vendor and paid for half a day. Getting through town, the traffic eased up giving both of them a relief with the wind hitting them. A rough and dusty road led the two of them to the secret beach and the closer they got, the more golf carts became visible. A big sign welcomed them to the secret beach. "We're here."

Sadie looked at the beach that seemed to be more crowded than any California beach "I think the secret is out."

"You want to swim?"

With a smirk and head shake she said, "Not really."

"Want to do something crazy?"

She drew back. "What do you call crazy?" He spun the cart around causing her to grab the handle and question his direction back toward town. Tightlipped he wouldn't answer her two hundred questions of where they were going but smiled when they pulled up to the airport.

"I have a friend with a plane." He grinned and headed toward a hanger.

She followed him excited to go flying but stopped before entering the hanger and studied all the posters of skydiving. "Wait, we are just going flying?" He disappeared into the office with her jogging after him. "Finn?"

"Do you trust me?" He pointed to a poster with his picture.

"I'm not sure." She cocked her head.

He pointed to another picture of the famous blue hole. "How about jumping into the world's most famous diving spot?" She stood speechless and paralyzed. "I used to help these guys out by jumping tandem. So, do you trust me?"

She nervously smiled. "Yes."

"Sweet, you only live once! Right?"

She stared at him, silent, with Paige's words now coming out of the mouth of the man she was falling in love with.

Go Slow

twenty five

What in the hell have I agreed to? Sadie pulled up her jumpsuit and zipped it. *I know I said I would be adventurous but jumping out of a plane?* She nervously nodded to Finn and walked to the plane. *Maybe I act like I twisted my ankle? Or in this case just freaking pass out!*

The plane started with the propellers spinning and a large puff of smoke; then it died. Sadie stopped and turned to Finn. "Is that normal?"

He laughed. "Yes. It's an old plane and takes a few times to warm up."

"I'm not sure . . . no, I am *sure* that I don't want to ride in an old plane!"

"That's ok. You're not riding in an old plane . . . you're jumping out of an old plane." He laughed again.

"Not funny."

"You'll be fine." He pulled her toward the plane.

Finn helped Sadie climb in behind four other people. "How are we going to get back here?"

"RK is coming to the island for supplies. He'll pick up his boat then meet us at the Blue Hole. Shorter trip to Caye Caulker than all the way back to Ambergris."

Sadie found a corner of the plane and pulled her knees to her chest leaning back on the wall. Two other girls were jumping with them "Are you nervous?" one of them asked her.

"Scared as hell!" She didn't hold back emotions. The girl laughed and agreed as the plane pulled forward, spinning around on the end of the runway. Finn smiled and gave her a thumbs up as the g-forces changed, pushing them toward the back of the plane it hurled down the runway. A couple bounces of the tires on pavement and the pilot pulled back and lifted the old plane off the ground and into the clear blue skies.

Sadie glanced out the window watching the island become smaller as the ocean grew. "Well it's all good now," Finn said sitting beside her.

"How do you figure?"

"We're in the air and we have a parachute, so if the plane went down, we'd be ok."

"For some reason that doesn't make me feel any better."

"I can make you a promise. It's an incredible feeling and you will love it."

Out the window, she saw Caye Caulker in the distance followed by island after island and then the barrier reef. Her world had been so big and so busy, but from above it seemed so small and idle. She thought about her life in Atlanta and wondered if she would be able to return. Then it hit her. *What are we going to do? Finn is grounded here with his place, brewery, and boat. I have my life back home or is it even home anymore? They said my world would change . . .*

She sat back with a different emotion, an emotion she came to the island to try and fix.

"You ok?" Finn obviously saw her expression change.

"Yea, just nervous." She lied to him for the first time.

The pilot turned to the people in the back and signaled two minutes by holding up two fingers. Finn moved behind Sadie and hooked his harness to hers; the pilot gave a one-minute warning and started banking to the left. Sadie tried to shake the depression that was returning but couldn't take her mind off what she had started with Finn. The pilot gave a thumbs up and the first couple entered the doorway and without notice jumped.

"You ready?" Finn yelled in her ear. She looked back and gave a halfhearted grin. The next couple positioned themselves in the doorway then leaped, leaving it vacant for Sadie and Finn. Approaching the doorway, she looked down at the ocean, reef, and a small dot that she assumed to be the Blue Hole. "3, 2, 1!" She closed her eyes and jumped.

Growing up as a kid, Sadie had been called a daredevil by her father and with a few trips to the ER for stitches, a cast for her left arm, and a sprain ankle, she agreed with him, but loved to hear him say it. As a father he had made many promises and had always kept them; he was the one person she felt the safest with, and never imagined life without him. Last year they received the news that his heart was dying causing her to grow a tremendous fear of not being with him.

Sadie opened her eyes and through the goggles she saw part of the world she never knew existed. Finn hollered and threw out his arms with excitement, her thoughts she had in the plane left and for the first time in a year, she felt free.

Attached to a man she was growing extremely close to, she realized she had the same trust in him that she did with her father. "Hold your arms out and fly!" Finn yelled.

She spread out her arms and feeling the lift of the wind she began flying and let out a scream of excitement. She never dreamed her month in Belize would put her thousands of feet above the ocean flying like an eagle. "Ok, sweetie, I'm about to pull the chute."

She looked back at him with a different expression, she wasn't sure why, but he sounded just like her father. After pulling the cord, her body joined with his, from horizontal to vertical with his hands gliding them in a swooping circle around the reef. "This is what living should be!" he yelled still excited.

The words he said, the tone he used, everything, it was as if her father was speaking to her through Finn. At a point where she should be terrified of falling to the earth with only a piece of cloth to save her, she experienced a feeling of safe, a feeling she couldn't describe.

"When we reach the water, I am going to pull back and put us in feet first, you are going to be pushed forward so don't let it scare you."

"I'm not scared," she said loud enough for him to hear. Watching the others hit the water first gave her an idea of what to expect. Finn banked them to the left and pulled back almost stopping their flight. The water on her legs was warm and after going under for a split second, she surfaced with more whooping from Finn.

With a smile no one could ease she felt Finn unsnap her and spin her around to face him. "Whatcha think?"

She started to speak but the words that came out were something she never thought she'd say to anyone she'd known for only a week. "I . . ." She stopped herself and threw her arms around him and locked her lips onto his.

She overheard one of the girls say to her instructor, "That was awesome, but I think we better just shake hands over it." She pointed to Finn and Sadie making out in the water.

twenty six

The next four days went by in a flash–helping Finn
at the bar, finalizing her design for Drifters beer, and
winning over B. She stopped going to the coffee
shop to avoid Lorene. Nights became longer,
mornings became shorter, and for Sadie, the coffee
in the office became better and better.
Conversations with Paige had become more
sporadic and her feelings for Finn more intense and
uncontrollable.

Sadie peddled down the sandy road that
paralleled the beach, casually waving at locals she
had met during her time on the island. Slowing
down and coming to a rest in front of the juice stand,
the lady behind the counter fixed her regular
pineapple, apple, and carrot juice without asking.
Taking her money, the lady wished her a blessed
day as she had for the past ten days. Sadie laughed
inside at the tourists that were figuring out how to

manage their bikes around the crowds and dodging kids and dogs.

The doors to the shed were opening with the sounds of machinery coming from inside. Looking in before entering, Sadie saw Finn hunched over his canning machine. Seductively she ran her hands around both sides of his waist expecting him to jump. Without movement he looked back at her. "You got to work on sneaking up on someone," he replied and went back to canning.

"I try," she answered in a chipper tone. "Can I help?"

"Nah, I'm almost done," he said not looking at her.

Sadie glanced beyond him at the pallet of stacked beer cans. "How long have you been working?"

"All night." Still looking at his machine.

"Are you ok?" She picked up on his tone and body movements. She waited for an answer but didn't get one. "Did I do something?"

He stopped what he was doing and faced her making her nervous. "You haven't done anything. I'm sorry." He pecked her lips and went back to work.

"Ok?"

"I do need a favor. Would you take this to B, she is at the bar." He gave her a small box of utensils.

"Sure. Do you want me to come back here?"

"Nah, I'll be there in a few minutes."

Throwing the small box in her basket she pushed off heading to the bar with mixed emotions. *Ok, so he isn't upset with me? What is going on with him? I wonder if Lorene is causing drama?* she thought as she made the short trip to the Split.

She set her bike in the rack, snatched the box, and jogged up the stairs. "B?" she yelled at the top.

"In here, kiddo." A voice returned from the kitchen.

"Finn said you needed this."

"Thank you. I'm not sure why our forks disappear as fast as they do. Why would anyone want a crummy fork from here?"

"Maybe they're accidentally throwing them away."

"Maybe, or maybe I'll find them when I find all my damn socks!"

Sadie laughed and poured herself a glass of water. "Finn was acting strange this morning."

Loading the forks in trays for washing, she said, "Yea, his father called him last night after you left."

"Is everything ok?"

"Who knows? He gets all weird when his father calls. Give him a half day, he'll be alright."

"Well, I was afraid it might have been me or something with Lorene."

B stopped at looked up. "Is that crazy bitch causing trouble?" She pointed a knife at Sadie.

Sadie's eyes widened. "No. Or not as far as I know."

"Good! I'd hate to have to cut her." She threw the knife back in the sink.

A loud thwack made both girls jump and spin to see Finn dropping two cases of beer cans on a table. They looked at each other as he ran back down the steps grabbing two more cases. "Do you want me to help?" Sadie asked.

"Nope."

"I'm sorry that your dad called. I'm not sure if that is bad?" Sadie said with B behind her swatting her with a towel and shushing her. "Was I not supposed to say anything?"

"No!" B gave her a dirty look.

Finn held up his hand. "It's ok. Apparently I can't tell anyone in my family what I am doing. My sister told my dad about Drifters Reef." He sat down.

B pointed at the four cases. "Those aren't going to cool themselves." She nodded toward the cooler.

"What's bad about that?"

"He loves the idea and wants to form a sister company with his and take the can that you designed and make it the signature beer."

She thought how that could be bad, then asked, "So why–?"

"He wants to run everything I do."

"But if he wants to help. . ."

He stopped her with a look. "Now he wants me to fly home this afternoon to talk about it."

"How long would you be gone?"

"I don't know. Two, three days." He flung himself up and started putting away the cans. "I don't want to be corporate!"

Sadie looked at B and shrugged her shoulders not knowing what to say. "Hey!" B blurted causing Finn look at her. "Take beauty here with you."

"Ah, you called me beauty." Sadie smiled.

"Don't get over excited, I call my cat beauty too." She turned to Finn. "Tell them you're getting married." Sadie almost fell off her stool. Finn stopped stacking and looked at her. "That would throw a monkey wrench in his meeting with you. Trust me, I know your mama."

"That's not a bad idea. You want to go to North Carolina this afternoon?"

Sadie shook her head. "Have you not seen movies about lying about marriage and introducing someone new to the parents? It never works out."

"I don't know about any movie but just bringing you home would turn the attention off the beer business and onto you. No marriage, plus you will love my sister and mom."

Sadie was speechless for a moment. "Can we even get airline tickets this soon? Wouldn't they be expensive?"

And in perfect timing a whistling noise followed by the roar of a small private jet flew over aiming at the runway on the north end of the island. "Not if your dad is persistent!" Finn pointed up.

"You're kidding?"

"B, hold down the fort. We'll be back in two days." He grabbed Sadie's arm.

"You got it," B answered. "Sadie?" she yelled catching her attention, "all those movies end with the girl falling madly in love with the guy!" She grinned.

A soft blushing smile fell across Sadie's face.

twenty seven

Sadie felt like she was in a movie when they arrived at the Caye Caulker airport. After rushing to her room at the resort and throwing a few things into a bag, RK took them to the small airport. Once there, a man dressed in a white uniform took her bag and waved toward the door of the jet.

Finn shook his hand saying, "Thomas. What happened to the last bird?"

"You know your father." He took Finn's bag.

Drawing in the smell of new leather and a hint of eucalyptus, Sadie made her way to one of the chairs that faced forward with a logoed blanket of the family brewery. A petite young lady walked out of the back wearing the same uniform as the pilot and offered Sadie a drink. "No thank you." She turned to Finn who took the offer for a drink.

"Yeah, I'm going to need it."

Within minutes the aircraft taxied down the blacktop runway and positioned itself for takeoff.

"Ready?" Finn glanced over. Before she could answer they were thrust to the back of their leather chairs as the pilot throttled the twin jets and quickly gained speed before pulling up. The island grew smaller three times faster than it did when they rode in the propeller plane just a few days earlier.

"Mr. Cantrell, we have clear skies ahead and should be on time." A voice came over the speakers. "Enjoy the flight."

"So, Mr. Finn Cantrell. Any other surprises I need to know about?" Sadie smiled, still dazed with her surroundings.

Finn picked up a remote and selected a track with piano music. "I'm not all rock n roll."

"Ok, I wouldn't have picked you as a Michael Curry fan."

"My mother will love that you know your Michael Curry music." Finn laid back and closed his eyes.

Sadie drifted off and even though she was in monumental bliss she fell into a dream with her father and a fight they had had years earlier, a fight that had haunted her. She had wanted to move to downtown Atlanta to be closer to her work and the night life that seemed fast and attractive, but her father wasn't ready to let go. Travis was with her at their house and tried to get her to reason with her father, but bullheaded and stubborn, Sadie moved to the apartment she lived in now.

The sound of tires hitting pavement and the jolt from the landing airplane shook her from a deep sleep. "I'm sorry. I didn't mean to sleep all the way." She looked at Finn.

"It's not that long of a flight."

"Well, I wanted to enjoy the luxury of a private jet."

He laughed. "You can enjoy it on the way back."

Sadie looked out the window at a black Expedition parked near a white stripped walkway. The jet parked next to the walkway and a beautiful woman standing at the end of it. *The Cantrell's sure have a lot of beautiful people working for them.*

Once the wheels came to a rest and the door lowered, she followed Finn out onto the tarmac. The young lady approached them. "You must be Sadie." Before Sadie could shake her hand, she wrapped both arms around her, hugging her tight.

Ok, they also have friendly employees.

"Ok, don't squeeze her to death." Finn pulled them apart.

"Let me guess, B told you to bring Sadie to keep Dad's mind of your meeting." She turned back to Sadie. "I'm Julie, Finn's sister."

"It's nice to meet you. I hope I am not causing trouble by coming?" Sadie replied.

Julie tucked her arm under Sadie's arm and headed toward the Expedition. "Are you kidding? My parents act totally different when we have guests. It will be a breath of fresh air to not talk about business." She looked back at Finn who carried their bags. "You still remember how to drive?"

Smirking, he replied, "Yes."

"Welcome to North Carolina." Julie opened the passenger door for Sadie.

The twenty minute drive from the airport to Brevard was filled with conversation between Finn and his sister. Sadie stared out the windows at the mountains in the distance thinking about texting Paige and letting her know she was in the States. But if she knew, she'd want to come see her. The vehicle began to slow down pulling into the city limits of Brevard. Sadie thought she was seeing things. "Is that a white squirrel?"

"Yep. Welcome to the white squirrel capital," Julie answered.

Sadie looked back at the small critter running up a tree. "That is the craziest thing." Then she noticed the street lamps with white squirrel flags hanging off them and a store named the White Squirrel. "Ok, what's the story with the white squirrels?"

"A circus came to town back in the 50s and one of their attractions were white squirrels. Long story short, they got out and multiplied," Finn answered.

Without answering, she continued to gaze out the window at the small downtown with shops, restaurants, and a couple of breweries. Crossing a bridge, she saw a sign that read *The French Broad River,* a river she remembered studying in history being the third oldest in the world.

Finn slowed and turned his blinker on, then merged on the shoulder before turning into a set of wrought iron gates held by a towering set of white cylinder block columns. Glancing forward into the immaculate landscape that welcomed them, she spotted a light-color mansion in the background. Winding along, she remained quiet and stunned at the enchanted grounds and the three-wing home they parked in front of. "

"Welcome to the Cantrell manor." Finn gently placed his hand on hers.

"Huh. I would have thought the heir of a brewery would have come from a nicer place." She laughed.

"I knew I'd like her," Julie said opening the back door.

The front doors of the home opened with an older couple walking out to greet them with hugs and kisses. There was no doubt they were Finn's parents.

"Mom, Dad. I want you to meet Sadie."

"Hello Sadie, it is so nice to have you here." His mother hugged her.

"Hello Sadie, I am Austin Cantrell but everyone calls me Butch." His father shook her hand.

"It's nice to meet both of you."

"Son." Mr. Cantrell turned to Finn. "I am glad you brought Sadie. Part of the reason I wanted to meet with you includes her."

"What?" Finn asked obviously confused.

"Other than your girlfriend, isn't she your marketing executive?" His answer caused two confused looks. "You did design the beer can for Drifters Beer?"

"Um, yes."

Finn took a deep breath and rolled his eyes. "Let me guess. You talked to Gary."

"A very persistent Canadian."

"Everyone wants their hand in," Finn replied.

"No business!" Mrs. Cantrell stepped in. "Sadie come with me, I want to hear all about your life in Georgia."

Sadie glanced back at Finn surprised that his mother knew where she lived, and the fact that his plan on bringing her to avoid business talk wasn't working.

twenty eight

Julie walked Sadie to the guest bedroom; a room larger than her entire apartment and left her to relax and adjust to their elaborate lifestyle. She looked down at her phone again contemplating whether or not to text Paige, when a shadow in her doorway startled her.

"Sorry," Finn said.

"You've come a long way from these slums," she teased him.

"I don't know. I'm still hanging around hoodlums and other troublemakers." He approached her.

Backing up she said, "You shouldn't talk about B and RK that way." She giggled before he threw his arms around her and lifted her off the floor. With one motion he tossed her onto the bed and quickly climbed on top of her pinning her arms to the mattress. "You're going to have to work harder than that if you're going to pin me." She

shifted her body and lifted her left leg over his back
and rolled out from under him and in another
motion, she pulled his right arm out pinning him to
the bed.

"Damn!" He laughed. "Now that you got me
watcha going to do?"

"I don't know, maybe I should think . . ." He
pulled her face to his and kissed her. She playfully
tried to pull back, but Finn's strength kept her lips
on his.

Ok, you win, she thought relaxing her body on
his.

She pulled her hair out of her face and noticed
a picture of Finn and Julie on the bedside table from
their elementary days. She laughed at the face he
was making in the picture. He pulled back. "Am I
missing something?"

She reached across him and showed him the
picture. "Is this the typical you?"

"Ha, yeah." He held onto her tight, obviously
not wanting to let go.

She felt his hands sink in her back pockets.
"Looking for something?" She gave him a funny
look. He devilishly grinned and ran his hands up
her sides and started pulling her shirt over her

shoulders. She pulled it back down. "Your parents are downstairs."

"So, I'll close the door."

She rolled off him. "You're going to have to show me around before I move to second base." She laughed.

"I hate baseball." He stood up. "Ok, come on. I'll give you the grand tour of Brevard and the National Forest."

They were halfway down the driveway in Julie's Jeep before Sadie realized she had left her phone on the bed. No doors and no top allowed plenty of wind to blow through Jeep causing her to hold her hair until she saw a red hair band wrapped around the gearshift.

Finn rested his hand on her knee sending little volts of electricity throughout her body. He began pointing to different structures and landmarks giving her the tour, but everything he said never was gone with the breeze. Sadie had drifted off in bliss watching his lips move.

"Well?" Finn asked drawing her from her daydream.

"Well what?"

"Have you been listening to anything I have said?"

"Yes." She grinned. "Maybe?"

"Where too?"

She laid the side of her face against the seat. "You're driving."

At a red light he said, "Fun, romantic, crazy, or educational?"

"Romantic."

"Very well." He spun the wheel to the right heading into the Pisgah National Forest. He tuned his phone to a station and Bluetooth to the radio; a station with indie songwriters and singers drifted into the air as they rolled through the mountains. Driving on the winding road, Sadie looked up at the plush covered cliffs that seemed to never end, a sight that was different from this morning flying out of Caye Caulker.

Her head in the same position on the seat she said, "I feel safe with you."

"You should." He put the Jeep in park. "Not many know about this trail. Come on." He leaped out.

Holding hands and half skipping up the trail they ran into a young family of four. The kids ran ahead of a tired couple who smiled and waved at Finn and Sadie as they passed. She could feel the trail incline slightly at first and gradually grow steeper with each step. Healthy vines and thick trees hung over the trail like a canopy creating a greenery tunnel through the thick forest. Rounding a bend, they heard laughter just ahead. "Not many people huh?" She tugged at him.

A couple of teenagers excused themselves jogging by and laughing. "Well," Finn took a deep breath, "I guess the secret is out."

They climbed farther and soon Sadie started to get out of breath. "I need to slow down." She panted.

"Yea, me too. I forget that I'm not in shape like my teen years."

Sadie took a couple of deep breaths and felt her pulse. *I'm ok,* she said over and over again in her head. "Should we have brought water?"

"Nah, it's not much farther. It's a short hike." He stopped and let her catch her breath.

"Ok." She pointed to the trail. Following him she pressed on pushing off her knees with every step and soon they walked out onto a flat rock with an edge that seemed to vanish into air. Breathing heavily Sadie walked closer to the edge to get the view of a small town resting below. *That wasn't so bad? Maybe I am in better shape than I thought.*

"My not-so-traveled spot seems to have gained popularity," Finn said with his hands on his hips, staring at a park trash can. "You want to go to another spot?"

Sadie sat on the edge. "This place is fine."

"Goodness, we need to get you in the gym. You ok?"

She patted the rock beside her. "I will be. Come sit." A welcome breeze blew and together they sat watching the busy town below. Finn talked about growing up in the community while Sadie listened and settled her heart rate. She had great thoughts of kissing and making out once they reached the place they were hiking, but now with sweat running down her back and still breathing heavily those thoughts disappeared.

"I feel like I am talking all about me. Tell me something about you I don't know," Finn said.

"I feel like you know everything about me," she lied.

"Where do you see yourself in a year?"

She took a hard swallow. "Hopefully with someone." He smiled at her taking the remark toward him. "Finn," she started again, "I need to tell you something."

Go Slow

His smile faded to a serious expression. And just as she started to speak again a group of people appeared on the rock with them.

Finn rolled his eyes. "I'll a pick a better trail on the next hike." He stood and pulled her to her feet.

She followed him holding his stretched hand staring at the back of his head. *This isn't fair; you deserve to know the truth.*

twenty nine

The door leading out to the six-car garage flung open with Finn and Sadie falling in, laughing about something that had happened in town on their way back. The kitchen was in disarray with pots and pans scattered across the countertops and sink. Pieces of vegetables, spills of spices, and a very fat dog littered the floor. Julie and Finn's mother jumped at the door flinging open. "I see you too have started the evening early." Julie smiled at them.

"Not yet." Finn opened the refrigerator and threw her a can of their seasonal lager. "You want one, Mom?" he asked.

"No thank you." She went back to cutting an onion.

Opening Sadie's beer for her he said, "Have you ever met a first lady of a brewery that didn't drink?"

Sadie felt guilty taking the beer from Finn in front of his mother, then Julie threw her arm around her. "So we have to drink for her." She touched her can against Sadie's.

"Can I help?" Sadie asked looking around the kitchen wondering what they were cooking.

"You can. Open those beans and rinse them off." Mrs. Cantrell pointed at two cans with the knife in her hand.

"Finn, while the ladies fix supper, why don't you come visit with me?" A deep voice came from the doorway.

Finn looked at his mother who said, "No business." She shot a glance at her husband.

Finn gave Sadie a funny smirk and followed his father.

***

Once in the dark glossy paneled room, the deep red curtains folded back from the windows allowing what little light that was left in the day. It was a room where Finn had received many lectures while growing up; college and business. He plopped down in a red leather chair that matched the curtains.

"Tell me about this Gary person from Canada." His father leaned against the mantel.

"Just someone who came to the bar. Why?"

"Seems everyone you meet ends up calling me wanting my business."

"Dad, you own one of the largest craft breweries. Everyone wants to do business with you."

"And what do you know about this girl?" He nodded toward the kitchen.

"You're too paranoid. She is someone I met on the island."

"Someone who is in marketing."

Finn stood. "Not everyone is after your company and money." He stood and started back toward the kitchen. "I brought her here to distract you from trying to convenience me to come back here to run your company. I see that isn't working."

"What's not working?" a low voice asked behind Finn. He turned to see Sadie with a half-smile, half-concerned expression. "I'm sorry did I walk in at the wrong time?"

Taking her hand and walking back into the kitchen, Finn said, "Perfect timing."

After taking one look at Finn's face his mother *harrumphed*. "He just wants his family here." She took off her apron. "And tonight, I have just that. My family here plus one very happy surprise." Sadie smiled obviously not realizing his mother was talking about her. "Supper will be ready in 45 minutes."

Julie cocked her head sideways and lifted an eyebrow. "Whatcha say, bro, rematch while Sadie watches me kick your butt?"

Finn's face lit up. "If my memory serves me correctly, I beat you last time."

Julie waved her hands toward the side door. Sadie wasn't sure what they were talking about, but she wasn't going to miss a brother and sister duel. They walked out to a basketball goal with a glass backboard attached to the roof of the garage.

"Don't let this change your mind about my brother." She covered her mouth so he couldn't see her talk, saying, "He sucks at basketball."

"If you're going to trash talk you don't need to whisper." Finn threw her the ball.

Sadie sat on the curb watching Finn and Julie play one-on-one, and with their energy and laughter she felt like she was in high school watching her boyfriend play. After Finn drove to the goal and scored on his first possession, he handed the ball to Julie who drove to her right then pulled up and hit a three pointer. Sadie's eyes widened.

Julie held up four fingers. "Started for NC for four years."

"Nobody cares about junior college." Finn started to take the ball out and with a quick hand and two steps, Julie stole it and put up another three pointer. Sadie watched as Finn was crushed 21 to 6 by Julie–someone she grew a whole new level of respect for and made a mental note to never cross.

Finn slapped the ball out of Julie's hand making it bounce in Sadie's direction. "Here you go." He held out his hands for her to pass it to him. Sadie stood and looked at the goal then back at him. "By all means." He waved at the goal. Sadie dribbled twice then took a shot that went straight in without hitting the goal.

She smiled. "Two years of junior college."

Julie jogged passed him and threw her arm around Sadie again. "Damn girl! If Finn doesn't marry you, I will."

Finn stood in shock looking at the goal and the ball that was still bouncing. "No crap?"

"Put up the ball little brother," Julie yelled as they walked in giggling.

The remainder of the night was filled with good food and laughter about the childhood of Finn and Julie and a story about Finn running away with a friend named Dylan. They played video games together and decided one day to run away to LA to participate in the world finals of Mario Brothers. After being spotted in Brevard, the sheriff picked them up and brought them back. Julie was crying with laughter explaining the story and their expressions riding in the back of the squad car.

In his defense she said, "Hey, they were pretty good at the game."

"What ever happened to Dylan?" his mother asked.

"He is one of the top chefs in Atlanta. He owns a place on East Paces Ferry Road. Ironically it's called Peaches."

"Serious?" Sadie looked at him. "I've eaten there."

Finn nodded his head. "That's Dylan's place."

"Mrs. Cantrell, supper was terrific," Sadie said.

"I'm glad you enjoyed it. You and Finn enjoy the rest of your evening."

"Oh, I'll help with dishes."

She shook her head. "No, you guys go have fun." She shot a glance at her husband. "I have help tonight."

Before anyone could say anything, Julie and Finn jumped from the table and with Sadie in hand, they headed to the living room. They flipped on a large TV and fell onto the couch like they must had done for years in the past. Sadie excused herself to her room and after taking a few wrong turns in the enormous hallway, she walked in to find her phone on her bed filled with text messages from Paige.

thirty

What the hell? I was about to load up on a plane and head to Belize, Paige's text read.

I'm sorry. I left me phone behind.

You said you would keep your phone with you at all times. Hence the reason for paying for international texting!!! And behind where?

Yes...Mother. Sadie rolled over and paused thinking about her next message she was sending. ***Oh yea...I'm in North Carolina at the present time***. She watched the phone for a reply, wondering if Paige was mad that she didn't tell her she was back to the States.

Her phone rang. *Great, let's see how colorful this conversation is going to be,* Sadie thought sliding the answer button.

"What the hell? You weren't going to tell me. Well, I'm on the phone now . . . spill it! What in the hell are you doing in North Carolina?" Paige's voice rang through the speaker.

"It was a last-minute thing that we flew back so he could meet with his dad."

"Last minute? What did that cost?"

Sadie took a deep breath. "Actually, his dad sent his private jet." She could hear Paige sit up from her couch.

"Private jet? Holy crap girl. Who is this Finn? Don't answer that. You better not screw this up."

"I really like him." She laughed.

"I would hope so. Are you coming here?"

"No, we are heading back first thing in the morning."

"Are you coming back here, ever?"

"I haven't thought past this evening yet."

"What's this evening?" Paige's tone turned to a seductive giggle.

"I don't mean that." Sadie shook her head.

"And don't shake your head. Have you made out with him yet?"

"Paige . . ."

A little knock from the door grabbed her attention. "You coming to watch TV?" Finn asked, poking his head in.

"Yea, let me get off the phone with Paige."

"Ah, your nosey friend from Atlanta. Tell her I said hi. And no, I don't." He turned back to the hallway.

"Don't what?" she yelled through the open door then turned her attention to the phone. "What did you ask Finn the other day on the phone?"

"Never mind that. You made out with him?"

"What did y'all talk about?" Sadie asked again.

"Never mind that. Spill it!"

Sadie took a deep breath ready for the river of questions. "The other night after a concert on the island . . ."

"The other night? Girl! You text me immediately on the cushy stuff from now on."

"Yes, Mother."

"But sounds like more of that is coming so don't keep your man waiting." Sadie could hear Paige laughing in the background as she hung up the phone.

"Paige? Hello? I swear you are like a freaking middle schooler!" She tossed the phone on the bed and left the room.

Hearing voices from the kitchen she stepped in for a water to find the Cantrell's playing like teenagers cleaning the kitchen. "Oh, sorry. I was just getting some water."

"Don't apologize. And make yourself at home," Mrs. Cantrell said still laughing.

Making her way back to the living room she could see her reflection in the dark mahogany floor with light casting off the flat screen TV that hung between two large palm trees. Finn was reclined deep into the leather couch with Julie's feet propped in his lap, a sight that ran the thoughts of her brother through her head.

***

Rushing through the halls of their high school, a young Sadie fought to hide her face from any lookers and questions as to why she was crying. All through her preteen years she had dreams of her freshman year being grand and filled with excitement of cheer, sports, and a social life. What she didn't expect was to be in a relationship with an upper classman who spread rumors about their sex life. The warm air pushed against her face with a fast-paced walk through the neighborhood toward her childhood home.

Go Slow

The front door exploded open, the sounds of her footsteps racing up the wooden stairs echoing before her mother could ask about her day. After the bedroom door closed behind her, Sadie dove headfirst into her pink satin pillow. The soft satin case soon became soaked with tears steadily pouring from her eyes. *How could he? And to the whole football team! I'll never go back there.* The thoughts flowed one after another.

"Honey? Are you ok?" her mother asked from the doorway.

"No. Please don't ask," she mumbled from her pillow.

"Ok, let me know if I can do anything." She pulled the door closed and walked back down the hall where Sadie's father must have been waiting.

"How's half-pint?" he asked in a jovial tone, his voice floating through the closed door.

"Not good. She's up there crying about something. I'm sure that boy." Her mother *tsked.* "But she wants to be left alone."

Ignoring her wishes Sadie could hear his heavy steps headed her way, a sound that never changed no matter his mood. "Hey, half-pint. You ok?" He walked in.

Sadie rolled over and faced him smearing her mascara over the back of her hand. "No. Why dad? Why are boys so mean, I thought they would have grown up in high school."

Her father smiled and shook his head. "Boys don't grow up until they have their own boys. You want to tell me?"

"No." She wasn't about to let her father know about the rumor her boyfriend, now *ex*-boyfriend, was spreading. She wasn't interested in visiting her father in jail from killing a dumb seventeen year-old jerk. But she wasn't going to pass the opportunity to curl up in his arms and cry it out. *Best dad in the world! Never questions me, just lets me cry,* she thought wiping her eyes.

The front door exploded with the footsteps of her big brother. "Sadie!" His voice rang through the hallways and up the wooden staircase.

"Sounds like your brother might know something." Her father smiled.

Heavy footsteps pounded against the stairs and ended at her doorway. "I took care of that jerk!" Travis proudly announced.

"Am I going to get a call from your principal?" their father asked.

"I don't think so," he reluctantly answered.

"I'll leave this conversation between you two." Her father kissed her on the forehead, patted her brother on the shoulder, then made his way back downstairs.

"What did you say?" Sadie asked.

"It's not what I said." He smiled and held up his right fist that was still red from punching the lights out of Sadie's ex.

"I don't need you fighting my fights."

"Bull-crap! No douche-bag is going to talk about my sister." He paused. "It wasn't true, was it?"

"No!" She climbed off her bed and wrapped her arms around him. "Thank you," she replied.

Her ex deserved it, but part of her was a little worried that her brother might have rearranged his face.

***

Finn turned to her and motioned for her to cuddle up beside him. The smiles from Julie softened her feelings of being accepted by his family. Sadie watched the reflections of the TV light bounce off and defines the facial features of Finn. She was entranced with the piercing colors from his eyes when he quickly turned, catching her off guard.

"You gonna watch the TV or me?" He laughed.

"You," she answered in a soft tone.

thirty one

Curled and sunk deep into a feather mattress, Sadie fought to keep her eyes closed, having one of the best sleeps she'd had in a long time. Her night had ended with a blissful kiss and the manners of a southern gentlemen. The light from a rising sun crawled along the glossy wooden floor to the king size sleigh bed where she curled in a ball staying warm. But after giving in, she pulled the satin curtains back to a view that overlooked the gardens that filled the back of the home.

Sadie peered into the mirror over the double vanity sink, running her tongue over her teeth thinking about her forgotten toothbrush, then looking at a tangled mess of hair. With thoughts of a warm cup of coffee she lightly stepped through the hallway when she overheard a conversation taking place in the living. *I'm not going to be nosy,* she told herself before hearing her name.

"Don't bring Sadie into this," Finn defended her.

"I'm only doing this to help both of you. You have a great talent and with her ideas of branding Drifters Beer you could be sitting where I am," his father replied. "She has a great resume with the company she works for in Atlanta."

"You're checking up on her?" Finn asked. "This is ridiculous! It's not always about the money. I don't need you to manage everything I do." He started out the door causing Sadie to quickly duck in the kitchen, still facing the living room intentionally keeping an ear open.

"There's more I want to tell you this morning." His father's voice rose.

"I'm done talking. We are heading back to Caye Caulker."

"Would you like a cup of coffee?" A voice came from behind Sadie.

Jumping, "I'm sorry. I just heard my name," she tried to explain herself to Finn's mother.

"Don't worry. It's nothing new for them to argue. And for my husband to try and run Finn's life," she replied shaking her head and pouring Sadie a cup.

"I swear. You guys wonder why I don't ever come back here." Finn stormed in the kitchen talking to his mother, then realized Sadie was in the room. "I'm sorry you heard all that. We are heading back this morning." He never stopped walking through the kitchen and toward his room.

"Maybe I should take him a cup," Sadie suggested but his mother beat her to the thought and handed her another cup.

Winding through the home and up a flight of stairs she came to Finn's room with the door half opened. Pushing it open she caught a glimpse of Finn disappearing into his bathroom, baring all. Her eyes grew twice their size and a teenage giggle came out seeing the muscles in his lower back and a butt as white as snow.

Tapping lightly on the door she said, "I brought you coffee."

Wrapped in a towel Finn opened the door wide enough to peak around and take the coffee. "Sorry this wasn't the trip you might have had in mind."

"Remember, you asked me to come here hoping that your father wouldn't talk business. But I got to meet your super cool sister."

"Yes, you did." He thumbed over his shoulder. "I'm gonna take a shower now." They stared at each other in an awkward moment. "Is that ok?" He broke the silence.

Snapping out of it, "Oh, yeah. Of course." She tried to laugh off the awkward moment as he closed the door.

Memorabilia from his high school years filled Finn's room, evidence that his mother didn't want to let go of her little boy. Glancing through the pictures of family and what appeared to be friends, Sadie's eyes moved to the clutter of medals and trophies of different sports he had played in school.

Finally she tipped toed out the door and back to her room to get ready and pack what little things she brought. Turning into her door a voice stopped her in the hallway. "Sadie?"

Looking back, she answered his father. "Yes, sir?"

"You are a very talented young lady in the marketing world," he started.

"Thank you?" She questioned where the conversation was going.

"Let me give you some helpful advice about Finn. Always be honest with him. That is the one thing I can say that I have been for him."

"Ok?" She still wasn't sure where he was going with the conversation.

"He's been hurt a few times and to be honest I am completely surprised he is falling this fast for you." Sadie just stared at him. "If you need any help, I know people in Atlanta who can help you. You don't have to walk through what you are going through alone." Her hands started shaking. "I just don't want to see Finn get hurt with you not being completely honest with him."

"I won't hurt him." She excused herself to her room disappearing into the bathroom and staring at herself in the mirror. "Wow!" Tears started forming in her eyes.

Retrieving her phone, she texted Paige.
Finn's father knows, she typed.

How? Paige answered.

I don't know. I guess he did his homework.

Well, it's not like you can keep it a secret. Maybe you should tell Finn.

No! I just need to break it off with him and deal with it myself.

Don't be dramatic, you like him. Maybe this is the way it's supposed to happen.

Sadie sat on the edge of the bed in deep thought not hearing or seeing Julie walk in her room

"You ok? You look like you just saw a ghost."

"No, I'm ok. Just talking with my friend in Atlanta about a problem she has."

"Oh, I'm sorry. Finn asked for me to drive you guys to the airport." She glanced around Sadie and seeing her bag unpacked said, "But take your time, it's the one good thing about having your own jet."

Sadie texted Paige and told her that she'd call once they made it back to Caye Caulker. Once packed, Sadie and Finn hugged his mother, thanked her for the hospitality, and one-arm hugged his father.

With instructions to call once they landed on the island, they raced down the driveway with Julie behind the wheel. Sadie watched the small town of Brevard slowly disappear on their drive to the Asheville airport.

"Promise me you'll stay in touch and definitely come back." Julie wrapped up Sadie, not giving her any room to hold her bag.

"I promise. Why don't you come out to the island?"

"That is a good idea." Finn kissed her on the cheek.

Julie nodded. "Soon. Promise."

With landing gear up and the pilot letting them know their expected time of arrival, Sadie sank back in the leather seat. "I could get use to this."

"That's good to know." Finn reached over and held her hand.

thirty two

White clouds drifted innocently above the Caribbean Sea as the Cantrell's jet pierced each one that hovered in its path. Sadie gazed out her window, watching the deep blue color of the ocean appear between clouds. She never felt the warm touch on her arm until Finn gripped tighter, pulling her around to meet his gaze.

"I guess I didn't do a very good job of distracting your father from trying to talk business," she said.

"Trust me, you did. He'd still be talking if you weren't there."

"Well, he seems like a great father. I'm sorry you don't see eye to eye with him." She glanced back out the window.

"Yea. Tell me about your father. You don't talk about him much–or you family at all, for that matter." After a long pause of waiting for her to answer, he said, "Or not." He sat back.

210

"One of the greatest dad's in all the earth," she replied still looking out. "Growing up he treated my brother and me so well. And my mother . . . like a queen."

"Brother?"

"He's older than me and has a beautiful family."

"Where do your parents live?" Finn asked.

After another long pause she said, "My mother left us when I was in high school."

"Oh, I'm sorry. We don't have to talk about it if you're not comfortable."

"No, it's ok. You need to know. My mother had big issues and blamed my father for everything. And one day, she threw her arms up and told him he could have the family and walked out the door. My brother and I weren't aware of what was going on with her until Dad explained that she was battling mental problems."

"Do you talk to her?"

"My dad fought to get her back home and get her help, but she refused. It was like she turned into another person having no emotions for the three of us." She looked at Finn with tears welling in her eyes. "She took her life four days after leaving us." Finn just stared in shock obviously not knowing what to say. "So, my father took care of us through high school and college."

"Where is he now?" Finn asked.

Tears fell in her lap as she tried to swallow once, then again, before answering Finn's question. "He passed away last year from a broken heart," she squeaked out.

He handed her a tissue. "I wish I had words."

"It's ok, I don't mean to be so emotional."

"Don't apologize. I would be a basket case too."

Sadie laughed through the tears. "I'm a basket case?"

"No, you know what I mean . . . I am just saying that . . . I don't know . . . maybe I just should shut up."

Sadie pulled her knees to her face and propped her chin on her knee. "It's fine. I *can* be a basket case from time to time."

"Can I ask how your father passed away?"

"He really did die from a broken heart. Restrictive Cardiomyopathy is the medical term." She wiped her eyes and nose. "He didn't know that he had it until it was too late to treat it. My brother and I just say it was caused from losing my mother."

"Wow. I just...wow."

"So, after losing him and a few other things going on in my life, I decided to get away for a month in Belize. I didn't expect this." She insinuated the private jet.

Sadie curled up in his arms and they watched islands appear on the horizon, a sign that they were close to Caye Caulker. What started as just flirting a week ago had turned into a deeper relationship, something that neither of them expected but didn't push back.

Sadie's ears popped as the jet fell from its altitude and the pilot tipped the wings at Drifters Reef as they buzzed The Split. B stood behind the bar shaking her head, waving a neon colored bar towel in greeting.

With a hard bank to the left, the pilot lined up to the runway and soon they touched down.   A red four seat golf cart waiting on them. Since Caye Caulker wasn't known for private jets to land there, a crowd of tourists and locals watched as Sadie and Finn stepped off like celebrities.

"Welcome back, your highness." RK smiled at Finn. "Madam." He took Sadie by the hand and kissed the back of it.

"A little too formal, don't you think?" Finn rolled his eyes.

Without notice RK swept Sadie off her feet and into his arms. "Would you rather me carry you?" He laughed.

Sadie laughed with him, in much need to change from a deep emotional flight back. RK set her down beside the cart and jumped in behind the wheel. "You're not going to help?" Finn asked carrying their bags.

"You got it covered," RK answered.

Finn looked at Sadie. "You can set my bags in the back." She smiled and sat in the passenger seat.

"Really?" Finn shook his head.

The air was hot but with the cart windshield lowered it gave them plenty of air as they made their way through the sandy roads. Sadie looked up at the jet roaring overhead, heading back to North Carolina.

"B will be glad you're back," RK volunteered.

"I doubt that. She seems to like it when I'm not around and can run it the way she wants."

"Well, you need to sell the bar to her and brew beer."

"I need to sell it to her plus the beer brewing and then sail away."

Sadie turned in her seat. "What's stopping you?"

"Two Detroit diesels and dry rot."

"Maybe the diesels but there's no dry rot on that boat," RK replied.

They stopped at the resort long enough for Sadie to put away her things then they sped to the bar for a night of island tourists, backpackers, and the evening's sunset.

thirty three

The following morning Sadie pulled the covers over her head and took a couple of deep breaths before emerging from her bed. The balcony door stuck for a moment but opened to a warm breeze. Rays of a rising sun and the sounds of gentle waves crashing against the sea wall welcomed her back to a place of serenity. She noticed the small office was open with a few other guests filling their coffee cups and water bottles. Sadie slipped into her flip flops and headed down with two cups in hand.

"How was North Carolina?" Tekka greeted her.

"Incredible," she answered pouring a cup then turning to smile at the very pregnant woman sitting behind the counter. "You're getting close."

"Not close enough, I'm tired of being pregnant." She fought to reach across her desk for a stapler.

"You're glowing too."

The compliment stopped her and created a smile. "Thank you, I needed to hear that today." Sadie stepped out of the way for a young couple to fill their coffee cups. "I see you're starting to get used to island time. You're sleeping till mid-morning."

"That might be the late nights."

Tekka smiled again. "I know. He even took you home to meet his family."

Sadie wasn't sure why she hadn't thought of it before but hearing the words from Tekka sunk into reality and with a wave of panic she thought, *I'm getting in this too deep. I'm not supposed to be finding someone here! I'm supposed to be relaxing and taking a break. Holy crap, what am I doing?*

"Are you ok?" she asked Sadie, obviously seeing her face turn pale.

"Yes, just tired. I am going to walk to the end of the dock." She excused herself.

Sand collected between her toes before she made it to the dock and after a few shakes she removed her flip flops. Thoughts began flooding her mind and, with little sleep and the need for caffeine she struggled to claim her thoughts. The young couple stepped onto the dock, arm and arm, coffee in hand, and expressions of happiness. Their actions and glances toward each other tamed Sadie's crazy emotional stroke.

"Good morning." The young girl spoke in a soft tone. Sadie put her in her late teens or maybe early twenties.

"Good morning. Newlyweds?" she asked.

"Not even 24 hours," the guy answered.

"You came to the right island to start your life together." Sadie smiled hiding her panicked state.

"That's great advice. And keep the island slogan close to you: go slow," Tekka said walking up behind them. "You left your second cup." She handed it to Sadie.

"Wow, how much longer do you have?" The young girl asked looking at Tekka's belly.

"This week." She grinned back and motioned for Sadie to follow her back. Once the two cleared the young couple, "Did I say something I wasn't supposed to?" she asked Sadie.

"Was it that obvious?"

"Call it a girl's intuition."

They strolled down the beach a little way staying within sight of the small office. "I actually came here to Caulker to take a break from life and now I find myself in a relationship after the first week. I'm normally a person who takes her time on life changing decisions, but I don't know what has come over me," Sadie started rambling.

"A beautiful island and a beautiful guy."

"I guess. You said something in the office just now and it kinda just hit home with me. I don't want to lead Finn on, I have to leave in a few weeks."

They stopped at two Adirondack chairs and sat down. "Don't let your mind complicate yourself. Don't make plans, just go with it."

Sadie sipped on her coffee. "Easier said than done. I'm not programmed to just go with it. I am a planner."

"So you planned to fall in love with Finn?"

"I didn't plan to fall in love . . ." She paused after saying the word.

Tekka patted her hand. "Love is a funny thing that nobody understands. Don't freak out, enjoy yourself, go slow, like you told that couple. It's a great place to start a new life." She glanced over and saw a man disappear into the office. "Come by the house today. I need some help cooking tonight's supper." She pulled herself up.

"Tonight?"

"Our weekly supper." She put one hand on her hip and managed her way back to the small office.

In the distance the waves crashed over the reef causing a continuous white line just under the horizon stretching for miles in both directions. Paige's words bounced through her thoughts; *You only live once.* And the advice from her father, *travel, meet people, and live.* She imagined her father somewhere in the clouds holding hands with her mother and acting like they were newlyweds. She had trained herself to only envision the good times with her parents and blocked out the last few years with them.

If I am going to continue to stay on this path with Finn, he deserves to know the truth about me. She looked up praying that the answer she was searching for would fall in her lap. The past year had been a life changer in so many ways; the loss of her father, her inheritance, and Travis. Paige had always been there for her and she missed her.

"If you look up too long a seagull is going to poop in your eye," a rough voice said behind her. She knew who it was before turning around.

"Good morning, B. What brings you to Anchor Resort?" Sadie greeted her.

"Tonight is supper night and I always stop by and see what I have to bring."

"*Have* to bring?" She grinned at B's toughness.

"Whatever. He's at the shed." She started to walk off.

"Do you want me to walk with you?" Sadie started to get up.

"Nope." B headed off.

Normally a rejection would hurt Sadie's feelings but after working with B for a week, she just brushed it off to normal B. Drinking her second cup she watched as B walked down the beach with arms puffed out and not moving off the path for anyone. The young couple sat at the end of the dock with their legs draped over the edge and feet dangling. Their playful touch and laughing made Sadie think about what she had with Finn, and with a strong breeze kicking up sand and small pine needles, her panic left.

Thanks Dad.

thirty four

Pedaling through the sandy roads Sadie waved at locals she had gotten used to while making her daily trip to the shed or Drifters Reef. Slowing to go around a few kids heading to school, she looked over at the coffee shop and saw Lorene behind the counter waiting on a tourist. She quickly ducked her head and pedaled faster. She wasn't in the mood to listen to Lorene gripe about losing Finn.

The sounds of shells and small rocks cracked and popped under the rubber on her tires as she stopped at a store to buy water. The double doors were propped up with rusted barbell weights and three fans drowned out the black and white TV behind the counter showing a Mexican game show. A nod from the elderly lady watching the screen was Sadie's greeting as she retrieved two bottles of water from a cooler in the back.

Three dollars down, Sadie stepped back into the heat and before she could place the water in her basket, a golf cart slid to a stop beside her. Looking over the rims of her sunglasses she saw it was Lorene and by the look on her face she wasn't happy. *Great.*

"Good morning," Sadie said.

"Cut the BS. You blow into our island and play this little miss innocent from Texas for what? A two week stand with my ex-boyfriend."

Crazy bitch from hell. The words echoed from B.

"First of all, I didn't blow into your island. Second, I'm from Georgia. And third . . . It's a four week stay, not two. Get your facts straight next time so you don't look like a dumb-ass!" Sadie bowed up. "And lastly, you need to remember the most important part: *ex*-boyfriend! Now leave me the hell alone."

Lorene stared back at her for a second then slammed her foot on the gas pedal, spraying rocks and shells behind her as she sped away.

"Freaking Crazy!" Sadie shook her head.

***

Finn leaned over wrapping a box in cellophane when a cold bottle of water went up the

back of his shirt. A dozen cans of beer hit the
ground, a roll of cellophane shot up in the air, and a
loud squeal echoed through the wooden walls of the
shed. Sadie's eyes widened before she doubled over
with laughter.

"What the hell? You trying to kill me?" Finn
took a deep breath.

"It's only water." She laughed.

"Sorry. My crazy ex drove by here three
times making me nervous. If I end up in the ocean
floating face down, you'll know who did it." He
took the water.

"I already had my run-in with Miss Crazy.
It'll probably be *me* that ends up dead in the ocean."

"What do you mean you had a run-in with
her?"

"She stopped me at the store and told me what
she thought about me."

Finn's expression changed. "I can fix that."

"No. B already told me that if I had any
trouble come to her. I know she doesn't want B on
her butt. And I took care of it. I told her exactly
what I thought about her. Now, you need some
help?" She changed the subject.

And with a nod and good morning kiss the
two of them boxed several cases of beer and stored

Go Slow

them in a walk-in cooler. Sadie pulled herself up on a couple of cases and watched Finn case the remaining beer as he talked about his plans for grilled lobster for their supper. His story slowly muted out with Sadie drifting off to a time when her father caught his grill on fire and had to call the fire department.

"Well?" Finn pulled her out of her thought.

"Well what?"

"Tonight," Finn repeated.

Sadie hopped down from the cases. "I told Tekka I'd come over and help her get ready. Do you need me at the bar?"

With a winkled face he said, "I just asked if you wanted to go get lobster with me for tonight."

"Oh. Well, I guess I don't need to be there till this afternoon. Don't you have to go to the bar? You are never there, and I don't want B to think it's because of me."

"First, I pay them well to take care of it and second, B *knows* it's because of you. Let's go get supper." He held the door for her.

The pros of living on an island is that being in a boat, any boat, is just minutes away and minutes later Finn and Sadie jetted across the waves heading toward his traps. The spray of the salt water from the hull pounding the waves had them soaked before they reached the first trap. Finn pulled back on the throttle and snatched a long pole with a hook on the end of it to pull up the first trap. With a couple of shakes, three lobsters fell onto the fiberglass floor and, once the trap was re-baited, it was tossed back in the water.

"What do you want me to do?" she asked.

"Hold open that ice chest," he instructed then wrapped on a rubber band to each claw with a contraption that was in his back pocket. He threw one of the three overboard. "Too small, I'll get him next year." Then he throttled down and raced to the next trap.

Pulling up to a glide he motioned for Sadie to take over the wheel and with the same precision as the last trap, he had four lobsters on the deck. "Keepers?" she asked.

"Yep." After two more traps they had twelve in the boat. "Well that's enough for supper."

"That was fast."

"Faster than going to the grocery store." He grinned.

I could get use to this, she thought spinning the bow toward Caulker. Finn fought with the last lobster on putting rubber bands on its claws, then fell toward the center console. He pulled himself around Sadie and ran his hands around her waist and held on. *I could defiantly get used to this.*

Sadie pulled up and sailed next to the dock. "You're getting pretty good at this. You need to quit your city job and become a boat captain."

"If only I could," she replied under her breath.

They tied up and with the weight of the ice chest Sadie grunted to get it onto the dock. With a bag resting on top of the ice chest they carried it together toward RK's golf cart. Sadie tried not to show that she was struggling with the weight and over-exerting herself. Her side of the ice chest fell.

"Crap!"

"It's ok. I can get it," Finn said.

Sadie shook her head in defeat and tried to follow him, but everything started to spin. "Please don't, not now," she said loud enough for Finn to hear.

"Not now what?" he asked.

Sadie tried to answer but the last thing she saw was him dropping the ice chest and reaching out for her.

***

Gently laying her on the dock, Finn yelled for RK but got no response.

"RK!" he screamed again. RK stuck his head out the old wooded door to the office and saw Sadie lying on the dock. "Bring water and a wet towel," Finn ordered.

RK raced to their side. "What happened?" He handed the towel to Finn.

"She just got over heated."

"You sure bro?"

"Yea, she'll be ok," Finn answered as Sadie came to.

thirty five

"So embarrassing," Sadie explained to Tekka while they cut up lettuce and celery over the sink in their house.

Tekka rolled her eyes. "Please. Embarrassing is when you pee on yourself because your baby is mashing on your bladder." She pointed to her stomach.

Laughing, Sadie said, "I guess so." She looked out the back window seeing Finn and RK standing around the grill drinking a beer and watching the lobster cook. The light from the setting sun behind them engulfed Finn, creating a halo around him and defining his muscle tone. A light shiver crawled up Sadie's back. "I have a question." She looked back at Tekka. "What happens if you go into labor here on Caulker?"

"It's just a ten minute flight to Belize City and a five minute ride to the hospital," she answered with no concern.

Huh, that's probably quicker than Atlanta, Sadie thought. The front door flung open with B walking in as if she owned the place. Her husband, who was seldom seen at the bar, closed the door and didn't miss a step heading to the back deck to join RK and Finn.

"Where do you want this?" B held a dish in one hand and the other on her hip.

"The refrigerator is fine."

"What is it?" Sadie craned up to see.

B looked at her and ignoring the question said, "You two need to hurry up and end this honeymoon part of dating and get your asses back to work." Sadie's eyes widen not knowing how to reply. "Y'all been jet setting, lobster hunting, and surfing all in… what… two weeks?"

Sadie wasn't about to correct her to only a week and a half. "We worked today at the shed," she answered.

B lifted her left eyebrow. "What did that take all of 2 hours?" Sadie started to defend herself but B held up her right hand. "Don't say it." She walked out to the back deck. "I don't want to hear about Finn's love life!"

Tekka laughed at B and went back to chopping lettuce and their conversation about her birth. A thought dashed through Sadie's mind about how she had gotten to this point and that she was happy for the first time in nearly a year.

"It's a damn good thing we only do this once a week; you three jackasses would drink up all the profits!" Sadie heard B say as she butted into the guys' conversation and pushed her way to the cooler.

"Yea B, it's a good thing." RK held up his can then clanked it against B's can, insinuating hello.

With instructions from Tekka, Sadie set an outside table on the back deck with plates, utensils, and glasses all sitting on floral place mats. The smell of grilled lobster engulfed the area making the group inch closer to the table with every sip of beer. Soon the sides began shuffling out the back door and set on the table.

The door swung back open with Toby and Shar carrying a large bowl of fruit salad. "Sorry we're late. My last SUP tour lasted longer than expected."

A few hugs from the girls and everyone found their place at the table and before they could remove napkins from plates, hot and steaming lobsters were sat in front of everyone. In a chair beside Finn, Sadie felt like they had been dating for years; the laughter, his arm around her, the group treating her like she belonged, the night could be any more perfect. Stories of each other spilled throughout the night, stories that had been told before but just as funny as told the first time. The story telling moved to roasting Finn to see how embarrassed they could make him in front of Sadie.

Finn held up his hands. "Ok, ok. I give, enough about me." Everyone laughed and like the wind changing directions, the roasting switched to RK. Finn pulled Sadie close to his mouth, whispering, "Thanks for being here."

"Thanks for pouring me a shot glass of ginger ale the night we met."

The night led to many beers, lots of laughing, and Bob Marley playing on the wireless speakers that lined the deck. RK was the first to lead his pregnant wife in an open spot and dance as close as he could without squashing the baby. Toby and Shar followed them to the dance floor and Finn coached Sadie to the open spot pulling her body close to his. Close enough she could feel his heartbeat, and hear him whisper thoughts that eight beers brought to mind.

Holy crap! How in the hell did I get here? Why is he so perfect? And why am I such a liar for not telling him the truth? Sadie's mind raced.

They danced to a slow song that heated the tension–not only between Finn and Sadie but the other couples too. All but B, who was sitting in a chair arguing with her husband about a professional basketball game that had taken place three years earlier. The song switched to a faster pace causing Finn to speed up his steps and twirl Sadie around the deck in a jitterbug, a two-step, and a few other dance moves she wondered if he could do sober.

The night went on for hours and with B and her husband being the first to leave, Finn and Sadie helped clean and then disappeared into the night on Caye Caulker.

"When are you going to buy your own golf cart?" Sadie asked Finn the same question that was becoming their joke as they bolted down one of the roads in RK's cart.

"Why would I need one? I got this one." They pulled into Anchor Resort and up to the stairs of Sadie's room.

"I'd ask you up but we need to get some rest. We need to help at the bar tomorrow." Sadie leaned in.

The left eyebrow lifted on Finn. "Let me guess, B was in your ear tonight?"

"Well . . ."

"Plus, how would you even know if I would want to go to your room? I'm not that easy Ms. Georgia."

"You are a southern gentleman, one of many things I like about you," Sadie said. *Damn! Where did that come from?*

"Oh really? What are the other things?"

"That you don't ask a bunch of questions." She leaned into his lips. "Good night."

"See you at Drifters Reef tomorrow." He peeled out in the sand and jetted out of the resort.

Sadie watched the taillights fade into the streetlights of Caulker then pulled out her phone, Face-timing Paige's number. "You ok?" Paige answered.

"Sorry, I don't mean to be calling so late. But I need to talk with you."

"Ok, what's up? Everything ok with Finn?"

"Is it possible to fall in love in two weeks?" Sadie stretched her time.

Paige smiled. "It's possible to fall in love in one sight. Don't get cold feet."

"I'm not." Sadie slowly made her way to the dock. "I feel like I need to be honest with him. We're getting close and I don't think it's fair to keep secrets."

There was a long pause on the phone. "I don't know, Sadie. I would wait and see where this is going. If it's just a four-week fling then he doesn't need to know."

"It's not a fling." She cut her off. "I really do like him."

"I don't know. I would wait another week. Things like this run off men."

"I'm feeling guilty. He's been nothing but a perfect guy to me." She sat down on the edge of the dock dangling her legs over the side, her feet feeling as heavy as her conscious.

Paige shook her head. "Nobody is perfect. Give it more time. One more week. What can it hurt?"

thirty six

Sadie pried her eyes open thinking she was dreaming of someone knocking at the door, but after another knock she managed to break out of her warm spot.

"Who is it?" she asked shivering from the cold air in her room.

"It's just me." Tekka spoke through the door.

Sadie unlocked the door. "Everything ok?"

"Everything is fine. Finn was looking for you and since I haven't seen you this morning, I thought I'd check on you." She held a steaming cup of coffee.

"What time is it?" Sadie asked.

"10 a.m."

"Dang, I guess I am getting used to the time here."

Tekka handed her the cup. "I'll let Finn know you're okay."

"Thank you. I'll be down in a few."

"Please, if I were you, I'd go back to bed."
She smiled and held her stomach as she headed
down the concrete steps.

After dressing, Sadie headed toward her
normal routine of walking out on the dock to watch
waves crash under her as she thought about life.
While holding the hot cup, footsteps closed in from
behind. Feeling the dock slightly shake and hearing
the creaking of every step Sadie timed it to when the
steps stopped and turned to face someone she wasn't
expecting, Lorene.

"I'm not sure why you are even bothering
with Finn. You should know that he is a one-and-
done type of guy," she said with her hands on her
hips.

"So, you were the one and done," Sadie
sarcastically replied setting her coffee cup on the
wooden pier.

Lorene took a deep breath and chuckled. "All
you American girls are the same. Trying to live in a
fairy tale story."

"Oh, I don't know. I think I have landed my
prince charming."

"I'd ask how he is kissing but I already know
. . . average." She smiled at Sadie.

"So, you've kissed so many guys you know how to grade them?" Sadie tried her best to hide that she was burning inside.

Lorene kicked Sadie's cup of coffee over the side of the pier. "Pack up and head back to where you came from . . . or else!" She turned and stormed off the pier and onto the hot sand that lined the water.

Sadie began to shake. She had worked so hard during her life to avoid confrontation and now she was in the middle of it. Her paper cup floated against the small sea wall at the end of the dock. She was so blurred with anger she never saw Tekka coming to her rescue.

"I know that wasn't a good conversation." She helped Sadie to her feet.

"Crazy heifer!"

"Yep, every island has one. Thank God it isn't me." She smiled, pulling a smile from Sadie. "Come on, I'll pour you another cup."

Sadie followed her back to the small hut that made their office. "What time is it?" she asked with her hands still shaking.

"Ten minutes since you asked me last time."

"Sorry, I am screwed up now. I'll see you this afternoon." Sadie jetted out the door and toward her room to change and grab her bike. Her mind shifted from Finn to Lorene then to her conversation with Paige the night before. So much so that she didn't remember finishing her coffee. With one person in mind she peddled through the small island like the evil lady from Wizard of Oz after taking Toto.

Passing the shed, she only vaguely noticed Finn standing the doorway. "Sadie?" he yelled.

Minutes later Sadie fishtailed her bike onto the bike rack at Drifters Reef and still in a forward motion, stormed upstairs to B. "That crazy woman kicked my coffee into the ocean!" she yelled.

A devious smile formed on B's face. "Ok? We have a few crazies here."

"Lorene!"

The smile left B's face. "What happened?" she asked as if it was an everyday occurrence.

Sadie spilled the story like a middle school girl complaining to her mother about all the mean girls at school. B, with hands on her hip, listened to every bit of the story.

"Finish stocking the cooler for me and put away the dishes and I'll be right back." She grabbed a steak knife and started down the stairs. Sadie watched her thinking maybe this wasn't a good idea telling B. Moments later B returned with Finn behind her, carrying the knife.

"Both of you sit," he demanded.

"You don't . . ." B started to reply but was quickly cut off by Finn. They sat down.

"Ok," Finn started, "yes, I dated a crazy from hell. Most guys probably have."

"I know my husband has," B replied then closed her lips after receiving a stern look from Finn.

"I wouldn't have guessed that she would come after you, but I will take care of it." He looked at Sadie then turned to B. "You know the hell we went through last time you stabbed a guy on this island?" B nodded yes. "Then stop it with the knives . . . or any other weapons."

Sadie jumped up. "She is evil and I can't handle her coming to the resort and–"

Finn placed his finger on Sadie's lips. "I know, I'll take care of it. What I ask from you is not to buy into her BS."

Sadie took a deep breath. "She talked about you guys kissing. That's something that a girl can't get out of her mind."

240

Finn shook his head. "I am not sure what to say about that. I know I can say that I never told her that I loved her."

Sadie shrugged her shoulders clueless. "Ok?"

"And I love you." He nodded toward her. At first it didn't register with her, then she felt the eyes of B glaring at her. "I know it's only been a couple of weeks, but I find myself in uncharted waters with you. I hope that doesn't chase you off, but I am serious about you." He stood up. "I'll be back in a few after I get this settled." He jogged down the stairs.

"Well holy cow jumping over the moon," B replied with her eyes still locked on Sadie.

Sadie sat in place as if shot. In a good way. "I'm not sure what to say."

"Welcome to your new home." B patted her shoulder then went back to putting away the dishes.

thirty seven

The sun had just set and the crowd made their way back to the bar from the sea wall, while Finn and Sadie steadily poured glasses of wine and mugs of beer. Finn had a strong reputation for brewing his own beer but there was still much explaining to new tourists, and Sadie was in the middle of explaining their Lime Gose when a man slapped the bar.

"Best damn beer anywhere in the world and I print all his cans!" Gary smiled from ear to ear.

"What are you doing back here?" Finn threw his white towel over his shoulder.

"Here to get the new drawings this young lady should have for me." He pointed at Sadie. She glanced at Finn with a deer in the headlights look, thinking she had dropped the ball on delivering her ideas.

"You know we haven't agreed to anything yet," Finn answered.

242

"I know, I was just picking on this young lady." Gary pointed at Sadie who took a deep breath of relief. "But I am here to win your business and get you a marketable can with her gift of branding."

"I'll tell you what, I'll let you two hash it out. Just don't spend all my money with this loud Canadian."

"Ha, we'll see about that. Get over here, Georgia, we have some business to talk." Gary waved her over. Sadie shook her head and laughed, bringing a cold mug topped off with Finn's Gose foaming over the edges. "You know how to start a meeting." Gary took the mug.

"You know Finn already has his beer Horizons printed," Sadie replied.

"I know, but this beer is what I want to print for him. What do you think of a lime and sombrero on the can?"

"You know Gose came from Germany." Sadie looked at him. Gary leaned back in his stool nodding with thought while sipping his beer. Sadie couldn't help but laugh thinking he was taking their meeting a little too seriously. "What about a cobblestone street leading through a small German town with the sun in the background as a lime?" She looked at him expecting to be shot down.

With one eyebrow up, he said, "Damn, you are good. I like it."

"I'll draw it up for you. How long are you here?"

"Two weeks!" He smiled.

Sadie didn't reply and figured she'd have plenty of time to draw up a design for Finn's next beer can. She snatched the towel from Finn's shoulder and wiped up the condonation from the frozen mugs and took an order from a couple of young Europeans.

During the night as they brushed by each other they smiled and playfully flirted with the words still fresh on her mind. *He loves me? Is it possible? Two weeks… is love at first site possible?*

Sadie sent a text to Paige and told her everything that had happened. She knew her response before it came back. ***You go girl!*** They texted back and forth until a loud group appeared at the bar hollering and ordering rounds for the crowd until Finn stepped in and saved the drunk guys money.

"Man, this was a crazy night," Sadie said to Finn later as they stacked chairs and picked up trash.

"Good night, you two." B stood at the bottom of the stairs eyeing them like they had done something wrong.

"Good night, see you later today," Finn replied seeing it was 1 a.m. He turned to Sadie, "I guess you'll just peddle back to the resort."

"Opposed to pushing it back? Or flying? Or maybe I'll get a running start and glide the length of the island." She laughed.

"You're starting to fit in with your smart-ass answers." He rolled his eyes.

She quickly slid in between him and the front of the bar that he was wiping down. "I was just kidding."

He drew back and cocked his head looking at her, and before she said anything else, he grabbed her by her waist and hoisted her unto the bar. His strength shocked her but not as much as when he ran his hands up her back and behind her neck where he pulled her head down to his. She could taste the salt from the ocean on his lips and before her goosebumps were gone, he picked her back up and gently sat her on a bar stool never unlocking lips.

With the sounds of waves slowly crashing against the sea wall and the eastern wind blowing her hair back, she sunk into a trance. At 1:10 a.m.

The Split was dead with people but alive with two heartbeats steadily bounding against the chest of two people quickly discovering each other. Finn's lips fell from her mouth to her cheek and slowly to her neck; she craned her chin upward with a rush of emotions flowing through her veins.

"I didn't expect this," she whispered. "But I am falling in love with you too."

Finn pulled back and locked eyes with her. "Stay with me tonight."

"I'm not sure I should."

Finn shook his head. "I'm not talking about sex. I just want to feel you when I wake up in the morning."

She thought for a moment. "Ok."

Her mind raced from what Finn had said; that there wasn't any intention other than just staying together. *What if something did happen?* she asked herself. *It's way too early.*

They strolled through the sandy road that led to his boat, arm and arm, content to be together. The boat rocked back and forth as they stepped aboard and the butterflies swarmed Sadie's stomach. The thought of sleeping in the same bed only weeks after meeting was starting to haunt her thoughts. So much that Finn must have noticed the expression on her face.

"Why don't I sleep on the sofa tonight and you can have my bed?"

"Finn?"

"It's ok, you don't have to explain. We are going too fast."

Holy crap, who is this guy? "I'm sorry. I'm leading you on," she replied.

"No! We are in this together." He walked her into his room. Hands on the side of her face he pulled her forehead to his lips and said goodnight.

Sadie pulled the sheets and comforter to her chin, sinking into a heavenly bliss with the smells of Finn surrounding her. The comfort of the bed, the muffle sound of the air conditioning, and 1:30 a.m. she fell into a deep sleep.

thirty eight

Sadie felt the boat move back and forth leaving her confused from a deep sleep. Opening her eyes, she was greeted by the blue water of Caye Caulker. She stretched her arms above her, realizing she hadn't moved all night. Sitting up she saw Finn through the back glass sitting in one of the fishing chairs. With the sheets wrapped around her, she tip-toed across the damp floor and out into the warm salty air.

Finn looked back at her. "Good morning, sunshine."

She smiled. "What time is it?"

"10:15."

"Whoa, I haven't slept that late since college." She awkwardly stood beside him.

With one swoop he pulled her onto his lap. He tried to be smooth but Sadie had already eyed the coffee sitting beside him.

"Do you have any more of that?" She nodded toward the steaming mug.

"Maybe."

She smiled and drew closer to his face. "One thing about southern girls . . . give us coffee in the morning."

"I'll take your word for it." He slipped out of the chair leaving her and her sheet. She quietly laughed inside and then thought about how many times Paige must have texted. It had become clear that Paige wasn't going to miss any news on Finn. For the last year Paige had begged her to date someone or at least go out with them, but it just wasn't something Sadie was ready for – until now.

A warm mug slid into her hands before Finn leaned back against the side of the boat looking out toward open water. Flip-flops, cut off blue jean shorts, and a ripped chest and abs caused Sadie to take a deep breath before trying to drink her coffee. "We have a few hours before we need to be at the bar, whatcha say we go scuba diving?" Finn looked at her.

"Uhh, doesn't that take a license or something?"

"I don't think you need to worry about the scuba police this early in the day." He smirked back at her.

"Finn, I don't know anything about scuba diving."

"I'll teach you, it's nothing. Plus we won't go deep. One of the great secrets to Caye Caulker is that it has the largest underwater cave in the Caribbean."

"I don't know," she nonchalantly replied sipping her coffee. "If I go, I need to go back to my room and get a few things."

"Like what?"

"Well for starters, a swimsuit."

"I doubt anyone is diving it today. What you have on is just fine." He devilishly grinned.

After a long quiet pause, he obviously knew that wasn't going to happen.

"I'll go diving another day. I need to call Paige this morning before she wigs-out because I haven't talked to her today." The morning was warm and with the buzzing of boats in the background heading out toward lobster traps, dive sites, and fishing, Sadie figured she better get dressed and head back. Downing the mug, she handed it back to him only to have him grab her wrist and pull her tight against his body. Nothing was said, just a sweet long drawn out kiss.

The night ran through her head followed by butterflies in her stomach like she had just kissed her first boy. Finn was perfect in her world, the problem was that Sadie felt a world away from him.

How is this going to work? she thought while peddling through the busy sandy roads of Caye Caulker. She was in such deep thought that she suddenly realized she was not on the road that lead back to Anchor Resort. She didn't see the rock in the road or her tire rolling over it. The sky appeared in front of her, then the road, then darkness.

Sadie pried her eyes open just long enough to see a man with dreadlocks leaning over her. "Hey lady," he called out. "You ok?"

"Agwe!" The man with the dreadlocks yells back toward the temple. "Agwe! Come here mon. This American girl crashed."

"Is she alive?" he asked.

"Yea, mon. But I think she is hurt badly," was the last thing she heard.

thirty nine

Finn finished an afternoon of canning beer. "Man, this is hard work for a measly pallet of beer," he said tapping on the walk-in cooler temperature gauge. A few cardboard flats fell his way before he heard the loud voice from outside. Finn shook his head hearing the overly loud Canadian greeting everyone as he made his way to the shed.

"Where's Georgia?" Gary stuck his head inside.

"Haven't seen her this afternoon. What's up?"

"Wanted to know if she came up with a sketch for your next number one selling beer."

Finn laughed then replied, "Since I am only one of three bars on the island it can't be too hard to have the number one beer."

"Ah, with your connections I can make you bigger than Budweiser."

"No thanks, I am happy right here in Caulker."   The humidity mixed with salty air made the door stick, Finn slammed it shut. "But I am sure she'll be helping tonight at Drifters Reef." He tried to hint that he needed to leave.

A hint that wasn't even close to being received. Gary hovered on the heels of Finn while they wound their way through the bicycles and golf carts streaming down the ocean front road. A strong wind blew across their path, temporarily blinding tourists and locals. Both Gary and Finn noticed the dark denim clouds racing toward the small island, churning the ocean to solid white caps and causing the street vendors to shut down early.

"That's impressive." Gary stopped in his tracks.

"It'll get here quicker than you think." Finn pulled the Canadian's arm and they picked up their pace to a steady jog toward The Split. Coming around the corner Finn saw B already lowering the storm flaps that covered the bar, knowing the blowing rain would soon be here. "I'll get the shutters." He glanced up at the restaurant.

The beach and The Split were filled with tourist taking pictures of the fast-moving storm, not having a clue that all hell was about to be lashed down on the small island. And after a crack of lightning belting down into the water just off shore and the first of the heavy rain, the tourists went running for shelter. B left the east side of the bar open to serve drinks to the group seeking shelter.

"Is this normal?" Gary's expression turned to worry.

"Yep, it'll be gone in twenty minutes. You can set your clock to it." Finn hopped over the bar to help B serve drinks. For the next twenty minutes the bar raked in money as the tight-fitting group celebrated the storm and toasted to anything they could think of.

"Where's Sadie?" B asked.

"I'm sure she's waiting out the storm before heading this way."

RK stood in the doorway of a store looking out at the rain and at the man jogging and dodging puddles in the road.

"What's your hurry, Agwe?" RK called out to the man.

"A white girl wrecked her bike in front of the place and she's hurt. Heading to the station to get help," he yelled back in passing.

***

RK thought a moment and realizing the rain was letting up he drove his cart to the temple, planning to offer a ride to the airport if the hurt person needed to be flown off the island. He knocked but with no answer he let himself in, "Hello?" he called out.

"In here," a voice answered him.

The Temple was small with only a few rooms leading into a living quarters. Managing his way through the dark rooms he ducked into a lit room with one of the men holding a towel over the forehead of the body of a young lady. "RK, am I glad to see you. Agwe just left to get help. This girl had a bad spill in front," he said in a thick accent.

RK stepped around him to get a better look at the girl. His heart stopped seeing it was Sadie. "Oh man, this is Sadie."

"You know her?"

"This is Finn's girlfriend."

Sadie's legs began twitching followed by a low drawn out moan. "RK, she's been out a long time."

RK fell to his knees and examined the back of Sadie's head where her hair was matted with dried blood. "She's got a serious cut. We need to get her to the airport and get her to Belize City."

"No worries, bro. I'll get our cart." He ran out of the room.

"Sadie? It's going to be ok. I'm going to get you the help you need. Hang on and we'll be at the hospital soon." Sadie's head slightly nodded back and forth giving RK some relief that she understood what he was saying. "I hope this doesn't hurt but I have to get you to the cart." He scooped his hands under her and lifted her off the couch and out the door.

Agwe came running from nowhere. "They have a plane ready," he said out of breath.

The cart started the half mile trek. "Tell Finn what is going on and we're going to Belize City!"

"Why?" Agwe yelled back.

"She's his girlfriend."

"Ah mon, I am not built for running." Agwe turned and jogged in the opposite direction, back toward Drifters Reef.

Before reaching the airport a green and yellow plane buzzed the tree line and RK knew it was for Sadie. RK instructed the man driving the cart to let Tekka know that he was flying to Belize City and would call soon. Sadie's eye's widened and blinked several times, locking onto RK's face, and the plane she was being loaded into.

"RK?" she asked confused.

"Yes. It's me. Just hang on and we'll be at the hospital soon."

"What happen?" she slurred.

"You had a bad wreck. Hang in there."

***

On the other end of the island Agwa ran up to the bar. "Finn, Finn, you here mon?" he yelled out of breath.

Finn came out of the back room. "Agwa, you ok?" he said followed by laughter.

"RK. . ."

Finn interrupted him. "They're having the baby?"

"No! RK told me to come get you. Your girl . . . she took a bad tumble on her bike and they are taking her to Belize City."

"My girl." Then it hit him. "Sadie?"

"Yea, mon."

fourty

Dark marbling clouds filled the western skies with an occasional flash of lightning; the same storm that had passed over Caulker. Finn braced himself against the cockpit wall with every bump the turbulent air threw at the single engine plane. He had made it to the airport just in time to catch a lift with the 5 p.m. flight from Caulker to Belize City. The only word he had received was that RK flew with Sadie to the hospital and that she was badly hurt.

Bad news or tragic news was something Finn wasn't accustomed to nor something he was sure how to handle. One part of him wanted to freak out but the rational part of him stood firm on keeping his demeanor cool and calm. At least on the outside.

Three weeks ago, he swore that he'd never date again with Lorene turning into a psycho from hell. He also never expected a small green-eyed Georgia girl to walk up to his bar. Now he had managed to take her home to meet the family, hire her at the bar, and tell her that he loved her.

"Hey, Finn. My friend is at the airport to take you to the hospital," the pilot, another friend of his, said.

He nodded a *thank you* back and watched the ground as they circled the one terminal airport. In the distance, just north of the airport, he spotted Belize's largest brewery, a brewery that made only two beers; but two very popular beers. The 20,000 square foot building reminded him of his father's brewery and a business that acquired countless hours, time he wasn't interested in. *You can have it,* he thought turning his eyes from the building to the runway.

After a couple of bounces off the blacktop runway with the throttle pulled back, they drifted in between two yellow lines and the pilot killed the engine. Finn climbed out. "Thank you."

"Hope your girl is ok. My friend who will drive you, is in a blue Nissan truck."

Finn jogged past the checkpoint and through the doors of the airport. A security guard tried to slow him down, but Finn was out the front doors and in the passenger seat of the blue Nissan before the guard could get to him. The streets of Belize

City resembled the streets and alleys of a third world country. There were three hospitals in the city. Two were nice buildings with trained personal and one had much to be desired in technology and modern medicine.

"Which one?" The driver asked.

Finn froze with the question. *Where would RK have taken her? Surely he would have gone to the private hospital with her.* "Try Belize Healthcare," Finn answered.

The truck pulled under a red and white awning next to the doors of the ER. Finn bailed out and stormed the doors. To his relief RK was standing at the check-in desk. Finn turned and gave a thumbs up and a wave to his driver before the doors shut.

"RK!"

"Hey man, she's ok. Hurt, but ok."

"Can I see her?" He looked at the nurse.

"What is your relationship with her?"

"Her boyfriend," he replied with a hint of questioning. It sounded strange and not earned as it rolled off the end of his tongue.

"You may go back, she's in room three."

"You coming?" he asked RK.

"Right after I call my wife."

Go Slow

The nurse pointed at a set of double doors with two small windows in each door. Finn glanced through them before slowly pushing them open. In the back he was met with a hectic array of nurses and doctors moving in a fast pace with plenty of patients to tend to. He ducked his head into room three to see a small bed with an IV tower, a monitor beside it, and Sadie covered in a thick blanket.

She lay motionless with a bandage wrapped around her head and her eyes closed. Finn tip-toed up to the bed not wanting to wake her and not sure how to act. This was definitely new to him and the staff hurrying everywhere behind him made him nervous. He placed both hands on the side of the bed, looking at the blonde locks that spilled over the bandage.

"You must be Finn?" A nurse asked walking in looking at the monitor.

"How did you know that?"

"Your friend RK said you'd be coming up here. Caye Caulker is nice isn't it?" She changed the subject.

"Yea, it's nice," he answered not interested in talking about the island.

"My husband and I try to get there as much as we can. But you know, work." She rolled her eyes.

"Beautiful girl you have here." Finn looked back her. "She's been mumbling your name since she came in. I'll tell the other nurses that the mysterious Finn has arrived."

"Is she going to be ok?"

"Well, she's been out for a while, but it's to be expected. Sadie has a nasty bump on the back of her had. No doubt she has a concussion, but give her a night and she'll be like new in the morning."

"She's staying overnight?"

"Definitely! The doctors will want to keep an eye on her. Plus, her heart monitor has been acting crazy. But I've seen this a thousand times, concussions cause some weird things. Who knows; she might wake up and not know who you are." Finn looked at her funny. "I'm just messing with you," she said with a chuckle while pulling the curtains.

"Finn?" Sadie mumbled out.

"I'm here."

"My head hurts."

"You took a bad fall." He took her hand in his.

"Call Paige," she said with a wince to her face.

"I will. Don't talk, just rest. I'm here." He patted her hand then noticed her cell phone on top of her clothes in a chair near the back wall. He texted Paige the short version of the story and within seconds Paige called. After assuring her that everything was ok and that he'd call first thing in the morning, he went back to holding Sadie's hand.

Thoughts flooded his head. *Why in the hell did I fall so hard for this girl? I hope I'm not setting myself up again for another fall.*

"Hey man, I'm going to catch a flight back to the island. You know, pregnant wife and all." RK ducked his head in the room.

"Thanks, bro." He gave him a one arm hug.

"You need anything, call me," RK said disappearing behind the curtains.

With CT scans coming back normal, the hospital moved Sadie to a room where Finn stayed by her side throughout the night. The traffic in and out of the room kept Finn awake and after pacing the room, he settled beside her bed rubbing the top of her hand.

"You weren't…" Sadie squeaked out with her lips barely moving.

"Weren't?"

She didn't answer for a while making Finn think she was talking in her sleep. Then, "You weren't supposed to fall in love with me… You need to know…" She fell back asleep.

Know? Know what?

fourty one

The following morning the sun kissed the horizon, the colors like any other morning on the island. Other than Sadie's head pounding and the room spinning from time to time, she was wide awake and inhaling her breakfast. Finn on the other hand looked like he had spent the night shooting tequila and fighting bears.

"Are you sure you don't want any pancakes?" Sadie held up a fork with three bites of pancakes dripping in syrup.

"No thank you. I have never seen anyone bounce back from death so fast," Finn said.

"I would agree." A doctor replied walking in carrying a clip board.

Sadie laughed then looked at Finn. "Would you mind getting me a cup of chipped iced?"

"Ok, I need to call B and let her know…" He looked at the doctor. "Will you be letting her go today?"

"Possibly, I just want to go over these–"

"I'm sure *we* are. Tell B I'll be back behind the bar tonight," Sadie interrupted the doctor.

"Ok?" Finn frowned as if he wanted to say more but ducked out the door.

Fifteen minutes later, Finn walked in Sadie's room just as the doctor was leaving.

"I wish you would reconsider, but it's your choice. Good luck to you," he said to Sadie then left.

Finn looked at the doctor then to Sadie. "Consider what?"

"Oh, he wanted me to do some tests. I'm fine and it's probably a money thing for the hospital since I have insurance. You ready?"

"Yep. We can catch a flight back."

"Let's take the water taxi. I need some fresh air."

"You sure? You probably need to rest."

Trying to hide the bounding headache, she said, "Words from the famous Paige: you only live once."

They hailed a taxi to take them to the water taxi dock. The wind from the open windows allowed the only relief from the heat, and Sadie laid her head on Finn's shoulder during the short trip.

They sat inside the ticket office in the air conditioning, waiting for the taxi. Finally, pulling out of port, they leaned back in their seats on the upper deck next to the captain. Finn and the captain talked like they were long lost brothers about a soccer team in Belize.

The ride was somewhat smooth for the forty foot taxi, crashing through the waves creating a wake and jetting toward the small island. Sadie fought through her headache to enjoy the colors of the water that glided with the deep blue sky. She didn't remember anything about her wreck or anything that happened afterwards. What she did remember was the night she spent on Finn's boat and the avalanche of emotions she was battling through about the man she had fallen in love with, the man she owed the truth.

The deckhand threw the weathered rope toward another man standing on the dock in Caye Caulker. Only four people exited the boat onto the sun-beaten wooden dock. The rope thrown over was never tied, just thrown back. Hand and hand Sadie and Finn started their way to the resort when a cart pulled up behind them.

"You two need a ride?" They turned to see Toby behind them.

"Man, you have great timing." Finn helped Sadie on first.

"You ok, girl? Word on the island is that Finn rigged your bike to fail and you wiped out."

She giggled. "Oh really."

"Yep. Where to?"

"Anchor Resort," Finn answered.

"Let's go to the bar. I don't want to be sitting alone in my room," Sadie said.

"You need rest."

"I'll crash on the couch in your office. I don't want to be alone."

Finn cocked his head. "Ok? To the bar." He pointed to his left.

A crowd of tourists and fishermen sat around the bar with only a hand full of people eating upstairs when they pulled up.

B examined Sadie's head and gave the best motherly advice she could. "Rub some dirt on it and you'll be ok."

But traveling back to Caulker in the heat of the day and boat crashing through the waves, had worn Sadie out. After turning on the air and turning out the lights, she crashed on Finn's office couch.

Through the closed door she could hear the crowd grow outside and, with the *oooohhhs* and the *awwwwes,* she knew the sun was setting. Sitting up, rubbing her head, she felt her phone vibrate in her pocket. A text from Paige. Knowing that she would write a book if she answered, Sadie called with her face-time app.

"Holy crap! I have been a freaking mess. What in the hell happened to you?" Paige answered the phone.

"I'm not as good of a bike rider as I thought. I crashed yesterday afternoon."

"Are you ok?" Paige's tone changed.

"Yea, I'm ok." Sadie tried to lie but the emotions for her visit to the hospital caught up with her and she lost it.

Paige started crying with her. "Damn it, Sadie. You can't be doing things like this."

"Doing things? Surely you know that I didn't do it on purpose."

"No, I just mean you have to take care of you. Do you need me there?"

Sadie wiped the tears from her face. "No, I'm ok other than a massive headache. Just talk to me, I need to hear your voice." And for the following hour they gabbed like teenagers about Paige's disastrous dates, Sadie and Finn, meeting his family, and most important, what was she going to do next week when her vacation ended.

Finn opened the door. "Everything ok?"

"Yea, just talking with Paige."

"If you're up to it, you have someone here to see you."

"Who?" Sadie asked puzzled.

fourty two

Leaning against the bar, gold bracelets bunched up on her wrist from her folded arms, stood Julie. Sadie blinked her eyes a couple of times then realized who was standing in front of her.

"Are you ok?" Julie gently wrapped her arms around her.

"Uh, yea." She peeled her back and looked at her. "What are you doing here? I mean I'm glad you're here, but…"

"Finn called Father for the jet in case you need to fly back to the States and I stowed away on the plane."

Sadie looked at Finn with a grateful smile. "Oh, he did."

"When was the last time you ate?" she asked and before Sadie could answer, she said, "Let's head upstairs and have B cook something for us." She smiled at B standing near the bar, looking unenthused.

"She does know that I don't work for your daddy," B said to Finn.

"Sadie should probably eat."

"I'll take care of Sadie, but it'll be a dead ass cold day in hell before Princess Julie flies here and thinks I'm some kind of damn servant." B stormed up the stairs.

The night was busy with a full moon rising from the west and a fresh bunch of Tennessee college students invading The Split. Bright orange became the dominate color for the night and the theme song of *Rocky Top* played a half dozen times, each time selling a round of drinks.

Julie and Sadie kept their table and seats long after the kitchen had closed. B left a bottle of sanitizer and a clean rag for them to wipe their table before they left and headed down to help Finn. The light from the moon gave white streaks to portions of the ocean mesmerizing the girls who propped up their chins on the wooden railing from upstairs.

"I've never seen Finn fall so hard for someone so fast. You must be a witch."

Sadie thought for a second. "A witch?"

Julie grinned at her. "You have a spell on my brother."

"It wasn't supposed to happen," Sadie answered turning her attention back to the moon.

"Well, it did." Julie paused. "You're perfect for him."

No, I'm not, Sadie thought, hoping Julie wouldn't pick up that she had a secret. But call it a sister's intuition, Julie picked up on something. Sadie's phone buzzed on the table catching both girls of guard and causing them to jump. They laughed and Sadie looked down to see that Paige was Face-timing her again. "I think she just got off a date, this is my best friend." She answered the call. "Hey, how was your evening?"

"Dickhead from hell! Why can't I pick up someone who is halfway decent? I swear, I attract guys who are stuck on themselves and want to be stuck on me."

"Boy, do I know that feeling," Julie replied.

"Who said that? Who's with you?" Paige drew closer to her screen.

"It's Finn's sister Julie." She turned the camera toward Julie. "Say hello."

They both awkwardly said hello at the same time causing Sadie to laugh. "I meant for Paige to say hello."

Julie picked up where the conversation had left off. "The last guy I went out with wanted to talk about my dad the whole time, how's that for a date?"

"Last month I went out with a guy who talked about his mother the whole night." Paige one upped her and with Sadie holding the phone, the girls had a five minute conversation about dating.

Sadie pointed the camera back to her. "Ok, I'm glad you two are besties now. But I am tired. I'll call you in the morning."

"Fine! Nice to meet you Julie, text me your number and we'll continue our conversation," Paige yelled in the phone. "Love you, dear. Please take care of you . . . and let Finn take care of you too, if you know what I . . ." Sadie hung up the phone with Julie laughing.

"I like her."

"Yeah, she's full of life."

The bell hanging over the bar rang and with a shout from B yelling last call, the lights turned off one by one. The natural light from the west kept a content glow on the beach. The girls remained upstairs until Finn climbed the stairs and collected them for the ride back to the resort, which, with every bump, made Sadie's headache worse.

"I'll walk you up." Finn took Sadie's hand at the resort.

"I think I am going to sit at the end of the pier for a while."

"You sure?"

"Yea." She kissed him. "You and Julie need some time to catch up."

Julie laughed. "I've had all the time I want with him. Plus, I am heading back in a few minutes."

Sadie hugged Julie and thanked her for coming to check on her, kissed Finn again, and slowly strolled across the beach to the pier with the Caribbean wind blowing her hair back.

Sadie sat on the dock with her legs dangling over the edge, something she had worked up to over her time on the island, fearing always something would come out of the water and bite her. Actually, it was more than fear leaving her, but the comfort of simply sitting on the edge of the pier. Her bike wreck had shaken her but mentally she was able to except that it was just an accident and could happen to anyone at any time.

Tears began rolling off her cheeks falling to the salt water below as an overwhelming wave of emotions came out. *This place feels right. But I*

*have a life back in Atlanta and Paige and I . . . I
don't know what to do.*

"Dad?" she said out loud. "I need some of
your advice. What do I do, I didn't come here to fall
in love. I don't even know if Finn wants me to stay,
he said he loved me but . . . what am I talking about?
I can't stay. You and I both know that." Tears
steadily fell into the water as she continued to pray
to her dad and sadly come to the conclusion that it
was time to tell Finn the truth about her life and say
goodbye.

She pulled herself up and took one last look at
the stars gasping the thought that this would be the
last time to see this view at night. Then a strong
wind blew past her with a whisper that only Sadie
could hear, "Travel, meet people, live!" The words
of her father, encouraging her to stay and give this
new life a chance.

Go Slow

fourty three

A loud knock from the open door of the shed caused Finn to jump. He looked over the pallet of empty cans to see B. "Where's Miss Georgia? She wrecks her bike and thinks she can have the day off?"

Finn wasn't sure if she was joking or serious. "I'm sure she'll be down before long. Kinda hard to give her hours since she volunteers at the bar."

B cocked her head. "That girl has you all messed up." Finn started to defend himself when she held up a hand. "No sense in answering, you are as hen-pecked as they come." Just then the roar from a private jet buzzed the island and made a hard bank to the right to line up for their approach.

Finn stumbled over a couple of boxes to get to the door to see what color the jet was. "Did you hear–" He started to asked B.

"Yep!" she cut him off and looked to the sky. "It's your dad's jet. Why is he here when Julie just left last night?"

"I don't know."

"Huh. Weird. You better go pick up your father at the runway. You know how pissed off he gets having to wait on you." And with a wave over her shoulder B marched to open the bar.

Why is my dad here? It was strange that their jet would make two trips in nine hours. But even stranger that he didn't let Finn know he was coming. He sped through the dirt and sand roads in RK's cart trying to get to the runway before the jet came to a rest on the tarmac. He cut down a side street lined with palm trees and other vegetation that hid the homes and apartments.

He turned in front of the small wooden building that represented their terminal and locked up the brakes on the golf cart in time to see the smoke from the tires of his father's jet hitting the blacktop. The pilot reversed the engines and taxied the jet into the parking area, something he had just done hours earlier.

Finn took a deep breath as the plane spun around and faced the runway, coming to a complete stop. Moments after the engines died down the side door opened and the stairs unfolded to the ground. He made his way to the foot of the stairs expecting his father to appear in the door, but it wasn't his dad.

Finn stood at the foot the stairs of his father's jet, much like a servant, trying to figure out who just appeared in the doorway. "Hello Caye Caulker!" The strange girl yelled. "I know that face." She pointed at Finn.

Finn bit his bottom lip before his jaw fell open. "Paige?"

"Damn right! Here in Caye Caulker in the flesh," she said in a thick Georgia accent, heading downstairs looking around him. "Where is my girl?"

"Ok, wow! Not sure what's going on. I thought you were my dad."

"Your sister is freaking awesome. She called me on the way back last night and told me to pack my crap that this badass jet was coming to get me and take me to see Sadie. And well, here I am." She hugged Finn. "I'm a hugger if you haven't figured that out yet."

Finn's eyes were wider than normal. "Ok?"

The pilot joined them, handing Paige her over-backed bag. "Finn, I am exhausted and going to grab a room for some sleep. If you need me, I'll be at the Anchor."

"Yes, sir. I believe we are heading there now." He pointed to the golf cart.

Once the jet was locked down and bags loaded, Paige climbed in the front seat. "Sadie is going to lay a golden brick when she sees me."

"I believe she will," Finn answered.

"But don't worry; I won't get in the way of you two."

Finn wasn't sure how to respond to that statement and didn't have time to worry about it.

Paige never stopped talking on the ride from the airport to Anchor Resort. "What a cool little island. I believe I am going to move here. You good with that?" she asked.

"I don't . . ."

"Yep, I am going to be an island girl. Go slow, huh? The island slogan." She waved at a couple of men lounging in the shade not giving Finn any time to talk. The pilot sat patiently in the back.

They pulled through the front entrance to the resort, and Finn spotted a figure at the end of the pier. "There's your girl." He pointed.

Paige went from Miss Chatterbox to Miss Serious. "Do you mind if I talk alone with her for a minute?"

"Of course not, I'll help our pilot get checked in."

The cart stopped at the office and Paige climbed out, heading toward Sadie and the turquoise blue waters of the Caribbean.

***

"You only live once," Paige said in a soft tone.

Sadie jerked around as if she'd heard a ghost and with the sight of her best friend, she leaped to her feet knocking over her coffee, wrapped her arms around her, breaking out into a long and painful cry. Paige's eyes filled up with tears, pulling Sadie close to her and for a long intimate moment, two best friends bawled their eyes out.

"I can't believe you are here," Sadie said with her head buried in Paige's shoulder.

"My best friend is in need," Paige replied.

"You don't know how bad I need you here. Thank you, thank you, thank you."

"Don't thank me."

"Thank you, Dad, I love you!" Sadie whispered to herself.

fourty four

B steadily cleaned the bar looking toward the road that led back through the small island, hoping to see Finn. It had been a long time coming that he would find someone he truly cared about. Now that he had, B worried it would have a negative impact on the bar.

The cook and a couple of employees took to their places and started the day; B took one last look at the road to see only a few local fishermen heading to their boats. "You guys get the restaurant started and I'll man the bar today," she said in a disappointed voice.

The Split slowly grew with people gathering in the water, laying along the sandy beach, and lounging under the table umbrellas that rested knee deep in the water. B tapped into a keg of Finn's latest batch and poured a glass for a young couple that had just arrived on Caulker. "You must be B!" A loud voice startled her from across the bar.

"I am. And you are?"

Reaching over the bar with her right hand, the woman said, "My name is Paige. I'm Sadie's best friend!"

B shook her head and quickly put together the return of his father's jet. "What you drinking?" She paused and restarted. "Wait! Where in the hell are Finn and Sadie?"

"They stopped for every person on the road. Me? I'm ready for a drink. Whatcha recommend?"

B wasn't sure what she expected from Sadie's best friend–especially a loud obnoxious friend.

"Beer." She poured another glass then slid it down the bar, still damp from salt water lingering in the air.

Paige spun on the stool that was permanently mounted to the sandy floor and gazed across the pearl white sand into the endless turquoise and blue Caribbean Ocean. A warm wind pushed her hair back and she inhaled a deep breath.

"So, how long are you here?" B asked.

Paige took a gulp from the once frozen mug. "Long enough to make sure my girl is ok."

B bowed up over the bar taking offense at the implication that she and Finn couldn't take care of a little Georgia girl. "And how long is it going to take you to figure that out?" she huffed.

Paige raised an eyebrow and replied, "About three minutes ago." She smiled and took another long swig. "Me on the other hand, I might have to hang out for a while."

B didn't have time to reply, and it was probably a good thing for Paige. Sadie and Finn walked up, holding hands and laughing about something.

"So, bartending is what you are doing on your vacation?" Paige said then looked Finn up and down. "I can see bartending." She giggled and took another swig.

B started to reply but came up empty and, after a moment of trying to come up with something to say, she just huffed, rolled her eyes at Sadie, then headed upstairs to run her restaurant.

"So, this is the beer you brew. Drifters Reef, huh? Are you the drifter? Or are you looking for one?" She laughed.

Sadie stepped into the conversation. "Do you need me tonight?"

He pulled her in tight and gave her a peck on the lips. "I've got this. Go show Paige the island."

Paige started to reply but was cut off by Sadie locking lips with Finn once more.

***

Sadie let Paige finish her beer, kissed Finn one more time, and dragged Paige off onto the sandy roads of Caulker. Paige talked the whole time, steadily running at the mouth about work, her non-exciting dating life, and the plane ride to the island. Smoke from the grills of street vendors filled the air with aromas of lobster, shrimp, and fish cleaned on the half shell. The girls tried each vendor's samples before landing in front of the lady that Sadie had bought lobster from before. Fresh lobster and small crispy red potatoes were devoured on site and washed down with two cans of Finn's beer from the lady's cooler.

"Damn, Sadie, I'm never leaving."

"Now you know. I still can't believe you are here in the flesh."

"We just have to find me a hot, tan, muscular, big . . . ."

"Ok, ok." Sadie quickly cut her off. "Sunset at The Split or swimming at the resort?"

"I'm ready for the ocean." And with that comment the girls ambled their way back to the resort.

The street filled with tourists, some heading to The Split for the sunset and others ducking into local restaurants for their last meal of the day and cold drinks. Stores remained opened in hopes of people purchasing items before heading home. The sounds of acoustics guitars flooded the street from hostels with drifters moving from one island to another. Paige stopped at one hostel and leaned against a sun-beaten porch column listening to a long hair, bare footed hippie strumming away on his beat-up guitar.

Well after sunset, the girls strolled into the gates of Anchor Resort and, walking in front of the well-lit hotel, Paige spotted the pilot on his balcony smoking a cigar. "What's up wings!" She yelled loud enough for half the island to hear. She received a wave that insinuated both hello and leave me the hell alone. She laughed and followed Sadie to her room. "What are we getting?"

"Swimsuits." Sadie gave Paige a funny look.

"Swimsuits? What the hell for, it's dark out there." She pointed toward the pier.

Sadie ignored the comment and opened her door to a cold room to change into one of the swimsuits that Paige had helped her pack weeks earlier. She glanced at her phone and noticed fourteen missed calls. *What the hell?*

She tapped the screen and saw that every call was from Travis. She held it up to Paige. "Why is he calling me? And why so much? Tell me you didn't call him about my bike wreck."

"I know, I probably shouldn't have but I was freaking out. You know if you don't call him, he'll keep calling."

Sadie closed her eyes and tilted her head back. "Well hell!" She hit his number and waited for him to answer.

"What in the world is going on? Paige called me and said you are in the hospital. Is this true?" Travis asked.

"I'm ok, I had a bike wreck and have a mild concussion. I'm safe and I am fine. Stop worrying about me."

"What are you talking about? Of course I am going to worry about you, I'm your brother. Listen, I am happy that you are seeing the world but it's time to get back here. Now. Is Paige with you? Put her one the phone."

Sadie's blood pressure grew. "You don't control my life anymore." She paused and took a deep breath. "Travis, please let me live my life."

"I can't help it. I love you and want what's best for you."

"Then let me go," she replied.

fourty five

Sadie heard the toilet flush and the sounds of bare feet running across the concrete floor of her room. Paige jumped in bed with her. "Holy crap it's freezing in here." She snuggled against Sadie and the warm spot in her bed.

It felt good to have Paige next to her, someone who was safe and like a sister. They faded back off to sleep until a soft knock echoed across the room. "Someone's at the door," Paige mumbled from under the sheets.

Sadie slipped into a sweatshirt, something she was glad she had with her room at refrigerator temperatures every morning. She cracked open the door to find Finn in cut off blue jean shorts, a tank top, his normal flip flops, and two cups of coffee. "Good morning," he said holding up the coffee.

With heavy eyes she said, "Give me just a second."

Sadie closed the door and disappeared into the bathroom to brush her teeth, somewhat fix her hair, and splash water on her face. She reopened the door and snatched the coffee, the warmth of the morning refreshing from her cold room, and glad Finn was there to greet her with coffee. "Did you stop by Lorene's?"

Cutting his eyes at her he said, "Please."

The sun began rising in the eastern skies of Belize waking the island with locals heading to work and fishermen boating to the traps and fishing reefs. Normally the dock at Anchor Resort was a place of serenity, but this morning Sadie was surprised to see a local's boat tied off and him standing at the end. She started to say something to Finn but he was already at RK's golf cart grabbing a bag. He jogged up to her side and smiled with the bag in hand. "Be right back."

He ran to the dock.

"Finn, mon, you didn't forget," the local said with a thick Jamaican accent.

"I'm not going to forget you," Finn said turning to Sadie and hollered. "It's his long day at fishing. I brought him a twelve pack."

"You a good mon." The man looked in the bag with twelve cold beer cans.

Sadie stood back watching Finn talk to the older fisherman then wish him well on his day of fishing, a trade that supported his family. And for some weird reason the sight hit Sadie with an excepted emotion.

Finn pushed the old man's boat off the dock toward the reef breaking several hundred yards out in the ocean. "What?" He looked at Sadie and her puzzled look.

"You amaze me at times."

Finn laughed. "Don't let giving an old man beer in the morning amaze you. He'll be lucking to get back to Caulker."

"You're good to people."

"They were good to me first."

Sadie knew that was just his reflex answer; she had witnessed him with locals and tourists, his demeanor never changed, he seemed to always put others first. She elected to remain quiet during the morning and listen to him talk about the bar, his beer that was brewing at the shed, and his family– mostly his father. It was a topic that he had become more comfortable discussing with Sadie and had been allowing her into what he thought was a dramatic family life. *If he only knew*, she thought.

"Hey," he said in a loud tone catching her off guard.

"Hey?" She laughed.

"You still owe me a Scuba diving trip."

"I do? I don't recall telling you I would go the first time."

"Perfect." Finn shot to his feet and grabbed Sadie's arm. "You're going to love the largest cave in the Caribbean. Kinda a little secret that only the locals and serious divers know about."

Sadie's eyebrows shot up with her concern; she had done plenty of sports but breathing underwater was a new one. *Isn't that dangerous?* she thought. But something about Finn in his tank top made her bite her lip and tag along. He had always put her first and she believed that he would never put her in danger.

After she went upstairs to tell Paige she was going with Finn for awhile, they rode in RK's golf cart, something that she had deemed as his, to a small dive shop on the west side of the island. They slid to a stop in the pea gravel in front of the shop with an old peeling mural of sea turtles on the outside. A thatched roof and broken shutters on the windows made her think if they kept their dive equipment in good shape. But again, *Finn would never put me in harm's way.* After a little convincing to the owner that she was a certified diver who had just forgotten her license, they loaded tanks, mask, fins, and weight belts in the back of the golf cart and peeled out heading south.

Finn went on about how the area hadn't had many divers and the reefs were practically untouched, virgin, and full of marine life. But if she really wanted to see the bottom side of Caye Caulker, this was one of the best ways to experience the island. They wheeled into a driveway and jetted past the house to the back of the property with a small opening in the brush of mangroves peeking out into the Caribbean. Finn said he knew them so it was ok.

"Finn, I don't really know about this." Sadie's apprehension got the best of her.

"It a shallow dive and the mouth of the cave is big enough for four tractor trailer trucks to drive through. Trust me." His pearly white teeth bled through his voice and suckered her into the salt water, into her gear, and under the blue water she had been looking at for the last three weeks.

They dropped down to ten feet and hung out for a short time allowing Sadie to gain comfort with her surrounding and the gear that she was strapped in. Finn held up the OKAY signal and she nodded that everything was fine.

He slipped his right hand into hers locking fingers, slowly swimming toward a dark blue spot that was as wide as a theater screen. The cave. All fears, all reservations, and all concerns left Sadie's mind with the opening of the cave painted in colors that only God could have created. Fish that she had never seen before welcomed her to their domain and as if the ocean accepted her as its own, Sadie swam in the most breath-taking environment she had ever witnessed. The sun light pushed through the water and lit most of the cave for the first fifty feet, illuminating the walls with green growth and smaller creatures.

A whole new world , she thought. Being able to experience it with Finn only added excitement to the dive that she would never be able to explain. They pushed through to the back of the cave with the opening only becoming a small dot taking in everything. She released his hand and swam to the top of the cave and placed her hand in the air pockets their bubbles were making, then a shadow caught her attention. A large fish slowly and methodically swam in her directions. It seemed to ignore their existence and aimed to the opening.

Go Slow

Finn swam up near Sadie about the time she realized it was a shark, and just not any shark but a very large shark.

She wasn't scared but rather intrigued; it displayed the demeanor that it was king of the ocean as it passed. Sadie swore it glanced at her in a respectful manner and like a priest, blessed her with the ocean and everything that came with it.

After letting the shark leave the cave, they made their way to the surface and breaking into the clear, clean air, Sadie removed her regulator. "I can't believe that."

"Beautiful, huh?"

"Un-describable. Thank you." She locked her arms through his and kissed him.

fourty six

Sadie lifted her scuba gear and tank into the back of RK's golf cart but before she could retrieve her fins and mask, a light-headed sensation swept over her body causing her to stumble.

Stepping around the cart Finn grabbed her arm. "Sadie? You ok?"

Please not now. "Yea, I think my blood sugar must be low. I probably need to eat," she lied.

He stared at her a moment, then shook his head. "Let's go get Paige and introduce her to fry jacks." He helped her into the front seat.

She raised her brows. "Introduce her? What about me? I don't recall you introducing me to something called fry jacks."

Finn grinned. "Well crap, I guess you're right. You are both in for a treat."

The wind pushing through the cart gave Sadie the relief she needed from the heat. She thought back on what she had just witnessed, the world that laid less than fifty feet below the road they traveled on. Her first dive was incredible and couldn't imagine being able to top it in any way. They pulled into the resort not expecting Paige to be up. But to both their surprise she had taken Sadie's place at the end of the pier watching the fishing and dive boats jet toward the reef breaking in the distance.

"I'm going to check on RK." Finn stepped toward the office.

The sight of Paige curled up in the Adirondack chair with her coffee pulled tight to her face made her smile. Sadie gently placed her hand on Paige's shoulder and without looking up said, "This is incredible. I now wish I would have come with you weeks ago," Paige said.

"Well you are here now."

"Where have you and Romeo been?"

"You're going to be pissed if I tell you."

"You ate without me?" She looked at Sadie.

"We went scuba diving in a giant cave under the island," Sadie said thinking Paige was going to go off on her for not taking her.

But to her surprise, "That sounds cool. But I am starving."

Sadie pulled Paige up to her feet. "Come on, Finn is driving us to get something called fry jacks."

Walking closer, Finn started shaking his head. "Well I *was*, but RK needed his ride. He said his wife wasn't feeling good and he was heading back to the house to check on her. So, we are on bikes."

Paige lifted an eyebrow. "Like bicycles?"

"You'll love it." Sadie locked hands with Paige on the right and Finn on the left. Moments later they had Paige on a bike and the three of them peddled to the fry jack stand like a bunch of middle schoolers. Finn and Sadie peddled ahead talking about their dive and planning the next one, as Paige struggled to keep her balance behind them.

"Now I see why you wrecked on one of the damn contraptions," she yelled to them. "If I wreck on this mother . . ." She hit a small pothole causing her to weave and catch herself by putting her foot on the ground. "To hell with this!" she yelled. A school teacher walking her kids to the small local school gave Paige a dirty look.

Sadie rolled her eyes. It was a toss-up whether Paige or B could be more outlandish.

Paige walked her bike the remaining two blocks. In the background stood a white shack with a rusty tin roof and a front porch that had a few tables. Sadie pointed to the shack next door for Paige. "Best fruit juice in the world, right there."

"How about a freaking water right now? It's hotter than the hinges of hell back here on these roads." Paige threw her bike against a light pole and walked up the steps to the porch.

Finn explained to the girls and a couple of ease-dropping tourists about fry jacks and their origin coming from a cheap meal that could be eaten any time of the day.

Sitting on the porch with very little breeze, along with Paige complaining of the heat, they devoured their fry jacks stuffed with beans and downed two bottles of water each. After throwing their trash away they stopped at the juice shack and bought three watermelon juices and then made their way to the main beach, and the wind they needed to cool down, but a golf cart with a frantic driver stopped them. RK.

"Thank God I found you. I thought I was going to have to drive out to the bar," RK said in a pant.

"What's wrong?" Finn asked.

"She's in labor and farther along than we would like. The next plane isn't due in for another thirty minutes. Finn, I don't think we'll make it and I was wondering . . ."

Finn cut him off. "My dad's jet is here and, yes, I can have the pilot take you."

"I stopped by the resort to look for you and I saw him and told him what was happening. He said to find you, but he would head to the airport."

Finn looked at Sadie. "You guys go ahead. I'm going to help RK."

"I just need your jet," RK replied.

Sadie pulled Finn to the cart. "We are going to see you two off at the airport." She turned to Paige "You want to go?"

"Nah, I'll head to the bar and wait on you guys. Congrats on the baby." She nodded to RK whom she had yet to meet.

The golf cart spun in a fish tail in the road and jetted off to gather Tekka and head to the airport, leaving Paige on the road to The Split.

***

Paige took a deep breath and slowly strolled to The Split watching the street vendors hassle other tourists buying their trinkets and other goods. The lady who had grilled her lobster the day before recognized her and offered her another meal. Paige shook her head but promised that she'd come back.

She went up to the bar to find B opening the flaps and uncovering the bar preparing for the day and evening. "Good morning, B."

"We don't open for another 30 minutes," B replied without looking up.

"That's ok. I'm waiting on Finn and Sadie."

B looked up. "They ditch you for some hanky-panky?"

"No, they took their friend and his wife to the airport to have a baby."

"No kidding! They are finally having it?" And with the end of her sentence Finn's father's jet buzzed the sky, banking toward Belize City. "How long are you here?"

"I don't know." She watched B struggle with a case of beer. "You need some help?"

B shot her a go to hell look. "Does it look like I need help?"

"I wouldn't have offered if I didn't think so," Paige popped off.

And with that B nodded for her to help move a few cases to get the bar ready. They swept the floor behind the bar, wiped down the counter, and straightened the chairs under the umbrellas.

"I see you conned Paige into helping," Finn said as he and Sadie walked up.

B looked at Paige stacking glasses then back to Finn and Sadie. "She's a smart ass heifer!" Then looked back at Paige. "Kind of reminds me of me." She looked back at the couple and said, "Don't just stand there! Get in here and help get this old run-down bar ready. You just come and go like you own the place." She climbed the stairs to get the restaurant ready.

fourty seven

The night started slow but picked up when word came from the national weather association that a possible storm was stirring a few hundred miles east of the island. Paige kept her volunteer position helping B. Being a regular patron in the night life of Atlanta she obviously knew her way around the bar, pouring drinks that even Finn hadn't heard. More and more guys flocked to the bar to catch a closer eye of both girls that seem to be naturals behind the bar. Finn monitored his cell phone waiting for RK to call with some news on the baby.

B came down to see what all the ruckus was about and slid up to Finn. "You going to exploit your girlfriend?"

"I think it's Paige they are wanting to see." He pointed to the Atlanta girl double pouring Margarita's and singing *Brown Eye Girl* at the top of her lungs.

"What is this I hear about a storm?" B changed the subject.

"Ah, you know this time of year. They blow up fast, move through, and disappear." Finn acted cool and calm.

"Yeah, you weren't here in '61 when Hattie hit."

Finn thought for a moment then looked at B. "You weren't either."

"Precisely! I avoided it then and I'll avoid it now." She headed back upstairs leaving Finn confused. Looking back at Sadie they locked eyes and with a soft smile and wink from her he knew she was having a great time. The sound of his phone ringing distracted him from Sadie and picking it up he saw it was his father's pilot.

"Hello," he answered.

"Finn, I have been looking at the weather and with this storm heading this way I think it would be best to move the jet back to the States. Call me if you need me back."

"I will, thanks for taking RK and his wife."

The line went dead leaving Finn with a funny feeling in his gut about the storm. It was too close to the island to have time to build up for a tropical storm or even a hurricane. But there were times that he would stare into the east during the night and see nothing but darkness and an empty ocean. The thought of a storm forming in the darkness into a destructive source sent chills up his spin. A secret that he hadn't shared with anyone was that he was afraid of the dark.

His phone rang again, this time it was RK.

"Is there a baby here yet?" Finn asked.

"Not yet but she's close. Just wanted to touch base with you. Have you seen the weather?"

Finn sensed a hint of fright in his voice. "I have but it will probably just blow through."

"I don't know, one of the weather guys said it is one of the fastest building storms he has ever seen. Can you check in with my staff in the morning and make sure they are getting ready for the storm?"

Finn laughed; RK's staff included two and a half people, depending on what day you showed up "Yeah, I got it. Now get back to the future mom." They said their goodbyes and hung up. The feeling in Finn's gut grew three times after RK called with his concern. RK had been in the islands his whole life and for a storm to rattle him it must be something.

"Is the baby here yet?" Sadie ducked in his office.

"Nope, not yet."

"Why was he calling?"

"Wanted me to check in with his staff," he answered and walked back out to the bar with her. His boat crossed his mind but with it docked on the opposite side of the island it would be fine—still there was always a concern. Finn entered the bar in time to see Paige lining up twelve shot glasses with a lighter in hand. "Hey!" He caught her attention.

Paige nodded with a grin. "Flaming Doctor Peppers." She lit the shot glasses filled with rum and the twelve guys on the other side of the bar dropped each of them into a mug of beer and turned it up.

"A damn good waste of beer brewed right here on Caye Caulker," Finn said.

Paige took ten dollars from each guy then looked at Finn with a hand on her hip saying, "One hundred twenty bucks in about thirty seconds. You here to patronize or make money?" She flipped her hair and went back selling another round to the guys.

"Yep." A voice came from behind Finn. "She is a spitting image of me thirty years ago." B laughed.

Sadie laughed, tugged at Finn's shirt to kiss him, then helped Paige rake in a record setting night for Drifters Reef. It was close to closing time when Finn caught Sadie by the arm and motioned for her to walk with him toward the east side of the beach, only two hundred feet from the bar. The wind had picked up tremendously during the evening only to excite the crowd more about a strong storm brewing in the distance.

Lightning had built up and now spider-webbed its way through the clouds and the darkness. "It is absolutely beautiful." Sadie leaned back against Finn who wrapped his arms around her body.

"Depends on how you look at it."

She spun to face him. "Should we be concerned?"

"Nah, I'm just not a fan of storms."

She snugged back against his body. "Don't worry, I'm here to protect you."

Finn chuckled and then took in a deep breath. He was holding a girl who he never thought it was possible he could fall for in a short time. And for the first time he was able to look past the darkness and meanness of a storm and appreciate the mystery and awe that it constructed as it barreled toward the small island. Lightning flashed through the sky and webbed around the ocean below, almost as if the storm was showing off for the couple. Finn pulled her around to face him. Their lips met in a sweet and innocent way—two people falling in love with each other. The air was pierced with a loud ringing; the bell that hung above the bar.

"Last call!" Paige yelled.

"I'm not sure I am going to be able to let you go," Finn whispered in Sadie's ear.

A warm sensation flooded her body. "Oh yea, why is that?"

"Free labor with you two. A bartender couldn't ask for more." He smiled teasing her and knowing that wasn't what she wanted to hear.

"Who said we were free? You haven't met the real Paige." She sinisterly smiled back and walked to the bar leaving him to question himself.

A low and steady roar of thunder moved through the island shaking everything that wasn't tied down.

fourty eight

Finn sent the staff from Drifters Reef home while he and B tied everything down–with the help of Sadie and Paige. The lightning grew more intense with the storm quickly approaching and, like a thief in the night, a strong gust of wind blew through The Split and whipped around all sides of the bar. Sadie looked at Finn with a hint of fear on her face, but he gave her a smile that everything would be ok. Paige tried helping B tie the last flap down but the cold beer in her right hand left her paralyzed to just her left.

"You know if you put that down, we'll get this done quicker!" B stood upright placing both her hands on each hip.

"I have never been to a bar without drinking and I don't want to start tonight." Paige held up her glass toasting B.

"Finn!" B shouted above the wind. "Lock up and get that skinny ass in the golf cart. We need to go!"

Finn smiled at B. "You think I have a skinny butt?"

She gave him a go to hell look. "I'm talking about her." She pointed to Sadie.

"Aw, you called me skinny." Sadie hugged B.

"Ain't got no time for that; y'all get in the cart and let's go." Her true southern accent came out when she was nervous.

Riding down the road B blocked the lashing sand from her eyes with her free hand. Locals scrambled to lock down their personal belongings, businesses, and anything that could be blown away. The tourists, the drunk ones, danced in the streets as carefree as one could be in an oncoming storm.

"Dumb asses!" B said swerving around a group.

The streetlights flickered a couple of times before going out and, like a row of dominos, all the buildings and homes went dark. The little island of Caye Caulker sat helpless in the Caribbean Ocean at the hands of God and Mother Nature.

B flipped on the headlights and aimed for the resort. As they rounded a corner, the hostel where

310

Sadie and Paige stopped the night before was lit with candles. Drifters crowded the porch singing along with the long-haired guy playing an acoustic guitar.

"Stop here," Paige yelled.

"What are you doing?" Sadie looked at her like she was crazy.

"You only live once." She smiled.

B looked at her. "What the hell?"

Finn, Sadie, and Paige all replied simultaneously, "It's Paige."

Paige stepped onto the sandy road and walked toward the porch. Sadie called to her again. "Paige, please come with us to the resort!"

Paige turned and smiled. "I'll be there later. You guys go. I'm going to hang out for a little longer."

Finn pulled Sadie closer, saying, "It's ok, I know the owner and a few people there. She is safe with that group."

B didn't wait for any reply and stomped on the gas, peeling out on the sand, heading toward Anchor Resort. The wind picked up, blowing debris across the last bit of road and as they pulled in, the rain began falling.

B dropped off Finn and Sadie, and pointed the cart toward her house. "It'll take one hell of a storm to ruffle these feathers!" she yelled as she was pulling away.

****

They raced up the concrete stairs to Sadie's door where she fumbled with the keys, allowing the rain to soak them before they pushed their way into the dark room. They both broke out laughing with wet clothes and still freezing temperatures in the air conditioned room. Sadie lit the room with her cell phone and Finn pulled his t-shirt off, exposing his ripped chest and abs taking the breath away. But her wet shirt clung to her body, and she wondered if the sight of it did the same to Finn.

She ducked into the bathroom to change before throwing him a towel to dry off.

"I know the electricity has only been off five or ten minutes but your AC works well," he said standing in the darkness.

Sadie stood in front of the mirror with her phone lighting the small bath. "Dang it!" she whispered. The thought that he wasn't going to his boat and that he was staying with her excited her and scared her at the same time. Then she realized she only had a dry oversized t-shirt with her.

Finn rubbed his head dry with the towel smiling when Sadie stepped into the doorway with the t-shirt on. "You are gorgeous."

The words brought a smile and blush to her face. "Thank you."

And like playing out in a movie she moved toward him, a movement that seemed to be in slow motion. The dim light from her phone and the sudden flashes of lightning outside highlighted their bodies as they faced each other in the cold room. Finn gently moved his hand over her arms and the goose bumps that covered her body. "You're freezing," he said.

"Yes." She giggled.

He reached down on the bed and pulled the comforter to wrap around her. "How are you going to get warm?" she asked.

"I better not get too warm. It might be a short drive to my boat, but it'll be colder than normal."

"You're not going back out in this!"

"I'll be fine…"

"No," she interrupted him. "You can stay here."

"I'll stay until Paige gets back. But staying with both of you would be kinda of weird and would have the island talking too much."

Sadie nodded, worried more about Paige than she let on.

fourty nine

On the other side of the island, the sun cracked the horizon disappearing over the mainland and jungles of Belize. The sounds of nature hadn't changed, the seagulls hoovered over the beach, the waves crashed over the reef in the distance, and the winds whistled through the weather-beaten lumber nailed on the side of the resort. What *had* changed was the debris that littered the beach, the front of the resort, and hung throughout the trees on the island. Indeed, the storm churned up to a tropical depression before striking the island, bringing minimal damage that could be fixed within a few days.

Sadie's balcony door opened, Finn stepping out to survey the area. "Man, that storm was more than I expected," he said.

The room was starting to heat up without AC. "Do you think Paige is ok?" she asked joining him.

"I am sure that girl can take care of herself."

And as if staged, Paige walked through the gates of the resort and waved at them standing on the balcony. "Speaking of the devil." Sadie smiled with relief.

Finn slipped on his flip-flops and waited at the front door for Paige to walk up. "I see you survived."

"I did but am I tired. They never went to sleep and we stayed up all night watching the rain fall." She landed on one of the queen sized beds in the room.

"Well, I'll let you guys have it. I need to go check on the bar and shed."

"I'll go with you. She'll sleep all day anyway."

Paige half-heartedly held up her right arm. "Go slow," she moaned through the pillow her face was stuck in.

Making their way through the streets, they were surprised at the damage from roof tops and beach furniture scattered throughout the area. Walking to the shed they passed the coffee shop where Lorene was outside picking up trash that had blown against her building.

"Everything ok?" Finn asked.

She raised up with a look on her face that said nothing would ever be ok, then she glanced at Sadie. "How much longer are you going to be here?"

Sadie snatched Finn's hand and locked fingers. "Oh, I don't know, but I promise much longer than you'd like," she answered with a snarl in her tone.

Lorene gave her a go to hell look and went back collecting trash.

"Dang." Finn cut his eyes at her. "I don't believe I have seen that side of you."

And as soon as Finn said that, Sadie realized she wasn't being herself. She would have never bowed up to someone back at home, she wasn't sure whether to be proud of herself or ashamed. While thinking about her reaction, they walked up on the shed where the walls were strongly intact, except where part of the roof had peeled off revealing the inside of Finn's small microbrewery. Within half an hour, a few nails and some swift hammering, Finn had them back on.

"There isn't any electricity! What is going to happen to all your beer?" Sadie said quickly forgetting about Lorene.

"Actually, I can hear my generator running. The cooler doesn't look hurt." He peered in the door at the soaked interior. "All this can be cleaned. Let's head to the bar." He closed the door.

They made their way down the street and up to Drifters Reef. Sadie picked out the sound of an engine running behind the bar. "Generator?" she asked.

"Yea, I have about three days running time of fuel. They'll have us back online by then."

"Thank God!" B made her way down the stairs. "Everything ok at the resort?"

"Yea, just minor repairs." Finn pulled out his cell phone and saw he had a small signal. He made his way to his office to call RK and check on his wife.

"Little Miss Atlanta ever come home?" B asked about Paige.

"This morning."

"Better keep a leash on her. This island is going to swallow her up." B laughed.

Sadie didn't have a chance to ask what she meant before Finn exploded out of his office and announced that RK and Tekka had their baby.

B stood on the third step and leaned around where she could see Finn. "On a stormy night too, I should have known that was going to happen. Grew up on a farm and those damn mama cows always had their babies in storms.”

“I don’t think there is any connection between storms, cows, and babies.” Sadie laughed.

One would have thought she threw a knife at B. “Now I know you just didn’t call my farm knowledge BS?”

“No B, I would never insult you.” Sadie stopped laughing and looked at Finn to jump in and save her. He just held up his hands and gracefully bowed out of their conversation.

The building shook as B stormed up the stairs and Sadie was able to take a deep breath of relief that B didn’t release a wrath of hell. She glanced at Finn. “Chicken!”

“Hey, you laughed at B’s statement. Not me.”

She repeated herself, “You’re still a big chicken.”

The rest of the staff slowly trickled in and helped arrange the tables, chairs, umbrellas, and start up the restaurant for a busy day to come. Finn’s was the only restaurant that had a generator and the locals knew that, but it didn’t take long for the tourists to figure it out. By lunch time the bar and upstairs were slammed with wall to wall people.

Sadie had found her groove behind the bar filling three mugs of beer at the same time, something she had seen at a local bar in Atlanta.

A bay boat with surf boards tied to the top rack fishtailed into The Split and came off its plane gliding up to the dock in front of Drifters Reef. Toby stepped onto the weathered dock, tied off, and made his way to the bar. "Hello Sadie, you heard the good news?"

She smiled. "RK's new baby?"

"Man, news travels fast around here."

Sadie poured him a beer

"You going surfing today? Kinda rough isn't it?" She nodded out toward the reef where they claimed a secret surfing spot.

"It's perfect today. Nice sets and plenty of barrels."

"I need to get you to take Paige and me out."

"You surf?" he asked.

"Well . . . I have before. We used to go to a small island called Tybee but I'm not really good. Paige on the other hand can do it all."

"Who is Paige?"

"A friend from Atlanta. She's here for a few days."

Go Slow

"I gotta take out some people today but you
tell me when and we'll go." He downed his beer and
spotted his clients. "Cheers!" He slid the empty
mug back to her.

fifty

The island had been through plenty of storms and was well prepared to restore lost power, clear the debris, and nail tin and boards back on that had blown off homes and business. Before the sun started its path into the distance horizon, Paige wandered into the bar.

"Well, I was wondering if you were going to join us today." Sadie smiled.

"I'm retiring from that side of the bar," she said loud enough for Finn to hear. Soon he turned to Paige motioning for Sadie to meet her at the end of the bar. "You're going to shoot me."

Sadie laughed. "You're going back to the hostel?"

"Yeah, but that's not it." She handed Sadie her cell phone and fourteen missed calls from a number she didn't want to see. Her expression changed. "Why in the hell is he calling me?"

She looked at Paige with a hint that she had something to do with it. Then she read one of the many text messages that Travis had left. Before she could finish reading, the phone rang with his name and number popping up.

Paige shook her head. "You might as well answer it; you know how pushy he is."

Sadie walked out of sight from Finn. "Hello, Travis," she half-heartily answered.

"Belize? Are you out of your mind? You need to be on the next flight home," he yelled through the phone.

Sadie shook her head. Travis had finally tracked her down.

"You don't control me, Travis," she replied not wanting to fight.

"Damn it, Sadie, you're being so hard-headed. You've had your vacation, please come home." His tone changed. "I don't want to be like this, but someone has to–"

"I have met someone," Sadie interrupted him in mid-sentence.

The line was quiet for a long minute. "You need to be on a plane heading back."

"Did you hear me?"

"Yea, I did. And I don't care."

"I'm not coming back," Sadie said catching the attention of Paige. Paige mouthed the words, *seriously*? "Let me make this clear, do not call me back! I don't need or want someone controlling my life. I mean it Travis, leave me alone!" She hung up the phone and before he had time to call back. Then, she turned it off, walked to the water's edge, and with all her strength threw her phone into the Caribbean.

"Oh, crap!" Paige drew back.

"If he calls your phone, it's going to be next." Sadie pointed toward the water. Paige slid the ringer off and gripped her phone. With hands shaking Sadie walked back to the bar then stopped and faced Paige. "You told him I was here." Her voice elevated above the music coming from the bar.

"He saw that I posted something about us on social media, then he called a couple of hours ago. I'm sorry."

Sadie wanted to be mad at her but it just wasn't part of her character.

"You ok?" Finn asked as he walked up, obviously seeing her expression.

"Yes. Just some problems back at home." She looked at Paige. "You staying?"

Biting her bottom lip and shaking her head she said, "Nah, I think I'm going to head back to the hostel and chill tonight. Are we ok?"

Sadie's shoulders dropped and she wrapped her arms around her best friend. "Yes, we are always good. I'll hang out for just a few more minutes then come join you."

Paige pulled back and looked at her. "No, stay with Finn. I didn't come here to take your time away from him."

"Still, I want to be with you. An hour?" Sadie asked.

Paige nodded. "Ok," then started her walk back to the hostel, a place Sadie would have never guessed would fit her. Paige had spent most of her life chasing her parents' dream of going to college, finding a career, landing a man, and settling down to have a family. The first two worked out well but finding the right guy had set out to be a bigger challenge than she ever dreamed.

About an hour later, Sadie ducked under some hanging ferns and scanned the room for Paige. With a simple wave from Paige she stepped passed a few people lying on the floor and sunk onto the bench beside Paige. She pulled Sadie in close to her and offered a glass of wine. At first Sadie was a little surprised that Paige had become drawn to a newer hippie group, but she remembered Paige's fantasies about joining a gypsy group and traveling the world.

"Where's your dude?" Paige asked.

"He said he wanted to give us some time and went back to his boat."

"Oh yeah, the famous boat. You'll have to take me to see the *Love Boat*." She elbowed Sadie. Both girls laughed then snuggled the rest of the night listening to the two guys play different folk songs. With her head on Paige's chest, Sadie thought about Travis and his persistence to control her life. It made her mad but in a strange way since she felt obligated to let him in on her life. He was her brother after all, the only family she had left.

"What are we doing tomorrow?" Paige asked.

"I don't know, we could go scuba diving."

Paige laughed "Don't you have to have a license for that?"

"Depends on who you know."

fifty one

The girls stayed longer than they intended and with several glasses of wine behind them, they headed back to the resort way of the beach. Sadie showed Paige a short cut that led through one of two cemeteries on the island. The wind from the east was stronger than normal and both girls' hair blew sideways as they stumbled and laughed their way back. Stepping into the light of Anchor Resort they sat in Adirondack chairs that nestled in the shadows of the palm trees that held four hammocks.

Neither saying anything and both lost in thought. Sadie was on a Finn-high wondering if he was sitting on the bow of his boat watching the same stars that hovered above the small island.

Paige reached out for Sadie's hand. "I don't want to leave," she said.

"Let's stay," Sadie replied with a glimmer of spark in her eyes.

"Could we? I mean what about work back home?"

"My job would only replace me with the next person. And if you're not going back then it would be an easy decision for me." Sadie couldn't believe her own words. Two months ago she would barely leave her house and now she was falling in love with a bar owner and the vibes of Belize; things were quickly changing.

"I don't know if I would want to stay just here on Caulker. I love the freedom and carefree life of those people at the hostel. What if I traveled with them for a few years? I could always come back." She faced Sadie with a different smile, something that Sadie hadn't seen before. "Holy crap! I am really going to do this. Is this wrong, I've only been here for two days."

Sadie glanced at her. "I fell in love with Finn in just one day."

Paige sat up. "I am so proud of you! After all the crap you have been through you have always kept your head up. And Travis, I never saw you bow up to him. Maybe now he'll see you really want a change."

Before she could answer, the sky lit up with a meteor followed by a golden sparkling tail that left remnants of its dust in the sky. The girls tightened their grip still holding hands. They had spent several nights on top of their apartment, a place they weren't supposed to be, searching the sky for falling stars. Now with a steady wind in their face and the sound of waves crashing against the small sea wall, they watched the sky littered with golden dust in hopes another would pass.

A warm light brightened the eye lids of both girls and the sounds of people walking to work woke them from their night. "Holy crap. We fell asleep in the chairs last night." Sadie shook Paige's arm.

"I'm going up to bed." Paige stood up.

"Coffee and fry jacks?"

"That sounds great, bring them to me." Paige stumbled toward their room.

Normally Sadie wouldn't be able to function after staying up all night, but she was wondering about Finn and after a splash of water on her face she hopped on her bike and peddled to his boat. With the motto of Caye Caulker in her head, Sadie went slow on her ride over to Finn's. She spoke with the locals who were already considering her a new resident and Finn's girl. Anytime she would overhear someone saying "that's Finn's girl" she would giggle inside like a middle-schooler.

With his boat in sight she could see the windows were wet with condensation much like her room back at the resort. After leaning her bike on a light pole, she lightly stepped onto his boat. Careful not to rock it she gently slid the glass door to the inside and entered the cold air that greeted her. She made her way down the steps and into his room where she saw the outline of a body under the covers. She slipped out of her flip-flops and crawled under the covers snuggling up to his warm body.

A moan came from Finn, then a sleepy smile when he cracked open one eye and saw her. He wrapped her up and with legs entangled they fell asleep, a deep sleep that could only come with two people falling for each other.

fifty two

Both Sadie and Finn felt the boat rock back and forth; the steps of someone on the stern. Finn rolled out of bed and pulled a t-shirt over his head with Sadie secretively watching him dress. She heard a loud, "Howdy. Hellloo, you two," from outside and climbed out of bed, knowing Paige wasn't going to leave.

Finn slid the door open.

"So, this is the infamous Finn boat? What's her name?" Paige barged in.

"Once she's running again, I will name her."

"What's the matter with you? Don't you know it's bad luck to have a boat without a name?"

"I already tried to explain that, but he wouldn't listen." Sadie emerged from down below.

Paige smiled. "Well look at you. Shacking up with the bartender, you ole slut." She laughed.

Finn shook his head slowly at Paige's sense of humor. "I have to fix the shed today and get some beer canned. Why don't you girls go harass the island?"

"We could get Toby to take us surfing," Sadie suggested.

"Hell yea! Where?" Paige asked.

"The waves break closer to the reef making for some world class surfing." Finn looked at Sadie. "I was hoping to take you."

She shrugged her shoulders. "Come go with us."

"I can't. You girls go have fun and have him drop you off at the bar when y'all are done." He pecked Sadie on the lips and gave Paige a high five on his way out the door.

After a quick stop by the resort to collect a bag of sunscreen, their bathing suits, and water they hoofed it for a juice and fry jack. When they emerged on the beach road, they saw Toby's boat tied to the dock. "That's a good sign, right?" Paige asked.

"That's a better sign," she said pointing at Toby asleep on a picnic table in the shade trees between the boat and surf shop. The wind was light with the noon sun shining straight down on the water creating a bright glare. Sadie shook Toby's foot. "You alive?"

He tilted his hat back from his eyes. "Sadie! And you must be the famous world champion surfer, Paige." He sat up.

"You going out?" Sadie nodded toward the water.

"Yea! My group canceled on me and I am just hanging for this afternoon. Let's grab some boards and shred some waves." He popped up and jogged to the shop.

Following him, Sadie introduced Paige to Shar. "You should come with us?" Sadie said.

Shar rolled her eyes at Toby. "Someone has to run the shop while the other is off playing."

"I'm sorry I didn't mean to take him away from . . ."

Shar interrupted Sadie, "Please, take him. I can get more done around here without having him lying around complaining that he's bored." She laughed.

Each carrying a board and Shar bringing an ice chest of water, they walked out onto the rickety old weathered dock. "Man, Toby, you better stay in line. Shar looks tough enough to whip you." Paige cut her eyes over to Shar.

Shar laughed. "I just look tough, soul surfer in here." She placed her hand over her heart.

"Well said. It was a pleasure to meet you. Maybe we can all grab a beer after this." Paige handed her board to Toby who was sliding them on top of the canvas roof.

"I'm down with that. Have fun." She gave them the hang loose sign and moments later Toby throttled down on the twin 250s and jetted north toward what he said was his 'favorite secret place.' During their thirty minute boat ride Sadie and Toby talked about the States while Paige sat toward the front of the boat soaking in the sun, the Caribbean Ocean, Belize, and the lifestyle that the girls had only ever dreamed of.

Toby pulled back on the throttle. "Ok girls, there are a few important things I need to explain to you about these waves." Paige joined them under the canvas tarp. "When the wave starts to break, the trough gets pretty shallow, so stay up on the wave and not in the bottom. Your fin could drag and toss you off."

Sadie stopped him. "Is this safe?"

"Oh yea yea, worst thing is you hit part of the reef and cut yourself but that is highly unlikely. I'm gonna keep you girls safe."

"I'm not a good surfer," Sadie reminded him.

"I know and I am going to help you. It's fun." He stopped the boat and walked to the bow to throw out the anchor.

Paige looked at the waves that were over a hundred feet away. "Why are we parking here? Can't we get closer?"

Toby laughed. "Park too close and one of you might run into my boat. It's just right there; you paddle farther than this on the big islands."

As Toby retrieved the boards from the top, the girls slipped out of their t-shirts and put on the rash guards that Shar had given them before they left. Sadie took a deep nervous breath and suddenly her world started to spin, she grabbed the console and placed her hand over her chest gasping for a breath of air.

"Sadie?" Paige grabbed her other arm. "Breathe slow and deep. Do you want a drink of cold water?" Sadie nodded and Paige let go of her long enough to fetch a bottle. Toby, not knowing what was going on, placed three boards in the water.

"I'm ok," Sadie said drinking a sip.

"We don't have to do this; we can go back in."

"No, I'm good."

"How often are your episodes coming?" Paige asked.

"Maybe two or three times since I've been here." Sadie worked to get her balance back.

"Your bike wreck, huh?"

"No, no that was a big ass rock in the road." She smiled.

"Alright girls, let's get in and I'll go over a few other things." Toby bailed off the side of the boat and into the water.

Sadie gave Paige a reassuring smile and they joined him for a perfect day on the waves. She hoped.

fifty three

Lying on their boards they paddled in the direction of a break in the reef that allowed waves from the east to pass by in perfect sets. Sadie looked over at Paige who was grinning ear to ear and obviously still on a high that only the islands of Belize could create. The sky was a deep blue canvas with white fluffy clouds that slowly drifted by changing shapes. Toby stopped and sat up on his board, the girls followed suit.

"This is where we want to stay." He pointed at the waves breaking in front of them. "Don't go over there or there." He pointed to each side of the reef about a hundred feet in each direction.

"Ok, it all looks the same," Paige spoke up.

"Looks, but isn't. For sure if you try to catch a wave in either spot, you'll drag the reef and it could get nasty fast. Here is good, safe, and never-ending. So, both of you have surfed, so you know the jest of it?"

"We got this." Paige started to paddle toward the break.

Toby grabbed her leash that connected her to her board and tried to stop her, but her ankle came un-Velcroed. "I see you got a board with a not-so-good leash."

"I guess so. Did you need something?" she asked.

"Watch the sets for a minute. You see you have about thirty seconds to cross the reef before the next waves comes. Be across it."

Paige saluted him. "Anything else."

He paddled past her in a hurry. "Yep, last one out has to carry the boards back when we get to the dock."

Paige grabbed his leash and pulled him back giving her the lead in the now-race to the waves. All three paddled their hearts out and, pausing only for a few seconds, crossed the reef in between sets of waves. Sadie nervously paddled looking down at the bright colors that lay below her board only a foot and half deep. As the reef started to disappear, a wave picked them up and crashed only a few yards behind them. Sadie was surprised how easy it was to cross over the reef and the fear and nervousness

Go Slow

quickly left. Now she was worried about wiping out.

Paige sat up. "Any other instructions or can we start?"

"It's your world, surfs up." He smiled.

Paige lay back on her board and looked behind her at the next wave that was coming. Sadie watched. Each wave seemed to be identical and, with arms deep into the water, Paige let the wave take her. Sadie craned her head to see Paige's hair waving behind her in the wind, and heard her scream something in excitement.

"I'm nervous," Sadie confessed to Toby.

"Don't be. If you think you're going to fall, lay back down and the wave will take you across the reef. Plus, if you did fall here, you'd probably be too far from the reef to hit it." He paddled and caught the next wave.

"Then why in the hell did you say all that crap about hitting the reef," she yelled.

Toby joined Paige—who was now obviously on a bigger high and ready to catch the next one, but they stayed—waiting for Sadie to join them.

Sadie took a deep breath. "Holy crap, why am I out here? Ok, I can do this. Paddle hard, let the wave take over, and pop up." She repeated her lessons from the summer she learned to surf. Looking back, she saw a wave coming that looked bigger than the rest, but she knew that was only her imagination. She wildly paddled and kicked her feet, that never touched the water, then once she felt the wave take her board, she popped up with knees bent and shaking like never before.

A bloody-murder scream accidentally left her mouth as she stayed balanced close to the board, touching it with her right hand to help her stand. She looked at Toby and Paige who were both yelling and waving fists in the air. Sadie had ridden her first wave in Belize and to her surprise— and no doubt Paige's— she didn't fall. After a few high fives they started paddling back out.

"You ok?" Paige asked her.

"I am." She panted. "Are you?"

"Damn girl, I am never going back. I am stating right now that I am an island girl," she yelled for everyone to hear.

For the following hour they caught wave after wave, challenging each other to see how far they could ride them, which was only fifty to a hundred feet past the reef before the wave would die down. Sadie was the first to wipe out but like Toby had told her, she was past the reef and never touched anything. Paige took a few falls trying to show off for Sadie and do moves that only seasoned surfers could manage.

At one point Paige talked Sadie into joining her on the same wave and with little persuasion they both paddled and popped up with cheering from Toby. They both rode the wave just before it died and Paige tackled Sadie off her board. They popped to the surface laughing. "Oh crap, my board." Paige pointed to where her ankle had come un-leashed again. She retrieved her board and joined Sadie for the trip back out to Toby.

Paige paddled ahead of Sadie and this time Sadie's timing was off and she got caught between waves over the reef. She felt her fin hit first then a stinging sensation from her foot followed with a stream of blood. She was under her board desperately clinging to it and clawing her way back up and away from the reef.

"Are you ok?" Toby yelled.

Sadie curled up on her board and saw a cut on top of her foot. "Yea, I just hit the reef."

"Don't put your leg in the water! Shark's will come!" Toby yelled back.

Sadie looked in his direction. "Sharks?" She looked at her foot that was slowly bleeding.

"Are you serious?" Paige asked Toby.

Laughing loudly, "No, I'm just messing with her." He caught the next wave and surfed in her direction. Pulling up and sitting on his board, he said, "Let me see." He motioned for her foot.

"Were you serious about sharks?"

"No, but I we should put something on it. Stay here." He headed toward the boat. Sadie took a breath of air in relief that he was joking about sharks.

"You big weenie!" Paige yelled over the waves at Sadie.

"Weenie? Surf your butt over here," Sadie yelled back, noticing Toby waving and hollering.

Paige was paddling for a wave that had taken her to the area he had warned them about. "No!" he shouted, trying to catch Paige's attention. "You're too close!"

Paige popped up. Her board tipped forward and jetted toward the swell that brightened with colors of the reef; the reef that was only inches below the surface. The nose of her board dug into the reef and launched her forward onto the reef and like an avalanche, the wave drove her deep in between two coral heads wedging her body into the sharp formation.

Go Slow

*****

At first Paige's thoughts were angry that she had done a stupid thing like drift into an area she was warned about, but her next thoughts turned to fear as she tried to free herself from the coral head four-feet below the surface.

She witnessed her board floating by Toby and then a wave driving him back as if telling him that he wasn't coming near her. Like a dream, where she couldn't scream or run, fear flooded her body. Toby fought against the next wave but couldn't get close to her.

Paige's vision, blurred by the salt water, caught glimpses of Toby fighting to get to her. In a panic she pulled against the coral struggling to free her foot but with each wave crashing over her, it drove her deeper in the reef until the last wave rammed her head against the coral.

Many people believe that their last visions of life would be with angels while others believe that everything slows down to a restful state. For Paige, her visions were of backpacking throughout the world, her family that she rarely saw, and her best-friend Sadie. The Caribbean Ocean is a beautiful and mysterious place, a place that draws people from all walks of life and gives them peace. Some for life and others from life.

This beautiful day with a backdrop of deep blue skies and perfect clouds the Caribbean Ocean took the life of someone who hadn't lived long enough. Paige's last vision was peaceful and beautiful.

"NO! GOD NO!" Sadie screamed as Toby finally freed Paige's foot and brought her to the surface.

Using a clean white rag Finn wiped the water from the bar as the fire department rolled up on The Split. The makeshift emergency room was close to The Split and the road made it quicker to get to the airport if someone needed to be flown to the mainland.

Finn ducked under the bar and joined one of the captains from the department. "What's going on?"

"Hey, Finn. We got a distress call that there was a drowning. We instructed the boat captain to meet us here."

"Wow! That's horrible," he said with B joining his side.

"Who called?" B asked.

The fire captain craned above Finn at the boat flying in his direction. "Toby," he answered walking toward the water.

At first the words didn't register with Finn. *Toby? Toby ... his Toby?* He knew that nothing could ever happen to Sadie, Paige, and Toby from the surf shop. Turning he saw the boat that had caught the attention of the fire captain.

"Oh dear God," B said joining the fire captain.

Everything— from Shar showing up, fire department personal, tourists joining out of curiosity, and his breathing—played out in slow motion. Finn locked eyes with Toby before they reached the seawall and he knew it was serious. He pushed past everyone and helped stop the boat from ramming the concrete wall. Sadie was in the bottom of the boat holding her best friend, frantically crying and begging for help.

"You got to let go of her," one of the firemen replied. Other firefighters climbed on the boat quickly strapping Paige to a backboard they had ready. Another person lifted Sadie, and Finn knew the moment she saw him.

"Help her, Finn, please help her," she begged.

"They are doing everything they can." He pulled on her and with the help from B they managed to get her out of the boat and over to Drifters Reef.

In the background they carefully loaded Paige's body onto the stretcher and placed her in the back of the ambulance; one of only two vehicles on the island. Shar and Toby stood helplessly near the other firemen. Sadie broke free from Finn's embrace, but before she could reach the ambulance to stop them, Finn caught her from behind and wrapped her up again.

Sadie's knees buckled and she slowly fell to the ground.

"I'm here Sadie" he repeated in her ear.

"Why, why Finn? It wasn't supposed to be her."

"I don't know."

"It's supposed to be me." She looked him dead in the face with tears flowing.

"Don't say that." He smoothed her hair, trying to console her.

***

"You don't understand." She stood back up and took a deep breath. Her body was numb and running off of adrenaline.

Toby and Shar froze at the boat when Sadie walked up to gather their bags, she halted for a brief moment then turned to Toby.

"Thank you for trying." She tried to add something, but her voice cracked and with crazy emotions she nodded in his direction to let him know it wasn't his fault.

In the boat she found Paige's bag pushed under one of the seats and, after picking it up, she sat down. Finn joined Shar and Toby at the boat. "I'm sorry, bro." He placed his hand on his shoulder.

"I tried to save her but the damn waves. . ."

Sadie interrupted them. "Can I ride back to the dock with you?" she asked Toby, but before she gave him a chance to answer, Finn said, "Come go with us." She looked at Finn.

"Ok." Finn looked back at B and waved letting her know he was leaving. The three of them climbed in and joined Sadie. The motor kicked off and slowly idled, pulling away from the shore. Sadie heard the bell ring and looking at the bar she witnessed B's hand pulling on the small rope attached to the small brass bell that hung over the bar. On a normal night B or Finn would ring it once for closing, but tonight B continued ringing the bell as if letting Paige's spirit know that she was loved and would always be honored on Caulker.

Sadie and Finn sat on the front of the boat gazing forward. "Do you mind going slow?" Sadie turned and asked Toby.

"Of course not. That's what we do best."

With dusk setting and the sunset hid by the island, the clouds that were white only an hour ago began to turn a reddish pink. Sadie stared forward still in shock not able to think.

"What is happening?" she asked Finn.

"What do you mean?"

"Where are they taking her?"

"They are probably taking her to the medical clinic. One of the firemen is the island coroner, he'll prepare her for a trip to Belize City before flying her body back to Atlanta."

Once back at the dock RK pulled up in his golf cart. News travels fast on small islands and he had received the news brief after getting back to the island with his wife and new baby. "Where do you guys need to go?" he asked Finn and Sadie.

"I guess to the resort to gather Sadie's things, she is staying with me tonight," Finn said.

Sadie wasn't going to argue and didn't have the energy if she wanted. They collected a few things for her to stay the night then headed to Finn's boat.

She walked out onto the bow of the boat while Finn spoke with RK and sat staring into darkness. A place she remained for most of the night. It was close to 3 a.m. before she joined Finn in the stateroom.

"I just don't understand," she said wrapping up in his arms and crying till sunrise.

fifty five

The fresh aroma of coffee filled the boat along with a hint of fresh baked cinnamon rolls. Sadie, still numb, lay in bed looking at the ceiling as thoughts returned from a confused night. She wasn't close with Paige's family but knew she needed to make a phone call, following their phone call from the local authorities. She managed to roll out of bed and make her way up the narrow stairs and into the main cabin of Finn's boat. She paused and heard voices outside.

"He is pretty shook up. . ." RK paused and glanced over Finn as Sadie stepped out of the main cabin.

"Toby?" she asked.

"Yea. How are you this morning?" RK asked then paused. "That was a stupid question. What can I do for you?"

She gently grabbed RK's arm. "I want to see your baby."

RK smiled. "That I can make happen."

"Let me shower and clean up first. Do you mind dropping me off at the resort?"

"Not at all."

Finn filled a couple of large cups with coffee and rolled up a few cinnamon buns for them. The guys sat in the front of the golf cart with Sadie slouching in the back. The island was well aware of Paige's death now and many locals waved. Older women blew kisses toward Sadie. In front of the coffee shop Lorene walked out and stopped the cart, with tears in her eyes she patted Sadie's hand then turned and walked back in the shop. A touch that no words could have ever topped and a touch that moved Sadie more than she would have expected.

Once they got to the resort, Paige looked at Finn. "I need to call someone, can I use your phone?" she asked Finn. He handed it to her and waited in the cart while she struggled to climb two flights of concrete stairs to her room. She took a deep breath and dialed Travis's number; it rang twice before he picked it up. "Travis?"

"Whose phone is this and why is your phone off?" he said.

"Mine is broke. . . Paige died last night," she squeaked out.

"I'm sorry, what?"

"Paige drowned yesterday evening." There was a long pause on the phone. "We were surfing and she got caught under one of the reefs."

"Let me come out there."

"Ok," she replied. She hated to have him come but he was the closest person to her and Paige, and could help with any arrangements that needed made.

"I'll head to the airport now; I'll be there before dark. How can I find you?"

"Just ask anyone at the airport, they'll know where I am." She hung up the phone before he could say anything else. The following phone call wasn't as easy as the first; she dialed Paige's father's cell phone.

The conversation was hard, with crying from both ends but the reassurance from her parents that they would be there for her in any way they could, made it somewhat lighter.

A light knock on the door and Finn poked his head in, she waved him in. After a quick shower and change of clothes, they locked hands.

Tekka opened the door, a tiny baby swaddled in a light pink blanket. For a short moment, tears changed from mourning to joy and though the day was heavy with tragedy, a motherly glow came from Tekka.

"Oh my gosh." Sadie's voice was soft. "She is gorgeous and look at you. You just gave birth and you are still beautiful."

"Sadie, I don't have the words you need to hear, but I bet this little girl has the touch." She handed her baby to Sadie. "The only other person who's held her is RK." She walked past the entrance and made her way to the living room and the couch, sitting down. Everyone else ended up in the kitchen giving Sadie time with one of the only things that can take her mind off of death.

"You are the most beautiful thing in the whole wide world and you have the best parents." Sadie talked with her before Tekka rejoined them. "What is her name?"

"Well, we haven't decided yet. We thought about naming her Victoria and calling her Tori, but she seems to be a little more fiery than that name."

"Whatever your name will be it will be the best in all the islands of the Caribbean." Sadie nestled her nose gently against the baby's nose. She smiled then latched onto Sadie's finger gripping as tight as a baby could.

They spent the majority of the day with RK and Tekka, and word got out on the island where they were. People began stopping by and dropping off food in condolence and celebration for the new baby.

"Hey, babe." Finn touched Sadie's shoulder waking her from dozing off. "I need to check in with B and the bar. I'll only be an hour or so. They want you to stay here."

She sat up. "I'm ok; I would like to go with you."

He nodded and pressed a warm kiss to her forehead.

They used RK's cart and, while riding through the main district of Caye Caulker, they noticed flags flying at half mass. The lady who was always cooking lobsters in the make-shift grill stopped them. "We locals are having a ceremony this evening at The Split to pay our respects to the spirit of your friend and to pay homage to the god of the sea. Please take this; food is everything." She handed Sadie a plate with four grilled lobsters.

"I am not going to argue, and I am deeply honored; we will be there." She turned to Finn, "I want to see her. She is still here, right?"

"Yea." He turned the cart around. A few blocks away they pulled up to the health clinic where a few people were waiting for treatment and to see the local doctor. Finn explained to the lady behind the counter who Sadie was and the lady disappeared through an old creaking door Moments later a man with a medical coat appeared.

"You wish to see your friend?"

"Please?"

"Of course, we are planning to fly her body to the mainland in a few hours where she'll be sent home." He smiled trying to feed her information.

This is her home, Sadie thought. She followed the doctor to a room where he entered first to prepare Paige for a short viewing. The door opened and he waved them in. Entering she found Paige wrapped in a white sheet and lying on a table with a glass of water next to her body, a cross submerged in it, and a lit candle. Finn explained that the Garifuna people of the island placed it by bodies to symbolize that the soul was still alive.

Sadie held her hand not realizing the coldness and spoke to her like she was still alive. She cried, she laughed, she yelled, and she said goodbye.

fifty six

That evening the local people began gathering at
The Split with flowers, torches, and beer from
Drifters Reef. A local native Garinagu lady took the
hand of Sadie and explained their ritual of burying a
love one. "We believe that the soul of someone
close never leaves and stays close as a guardian. We
will pray for her soul for nine days. Some of these
people are Mayan, like your friend Toby and his
wife Shar, and have many different gods." She
smiled at Sadie. "Honestly things have changed so
much that it's all a mixture of different cultures and
a little of that Christian stuff. Our main purpose is
to honor your friend." She gave Sadie a red rose.
"You will need to say something before tossing this
into the ocean."

On any normal day or night, speaking in front
of a crowd would terrify her, but this crowd was
different, this crowd was family. The elders each
took a few minutes and spoke, not only of Paige but

of community and the importance of staying together, staying around people. It was unlike any funeral or memorial she had ever attended.

Her time came to speak. With Finn by her side she stood between the ocean and the crowd.

"Paige was the friend who always seemed to make me mad but always made me laugh at the same time. She was full of love and life and was never scared of anything. Always a role model and always a big sister. She had full intentions of leaving her life back in the States and traveling with a group that she was quickly falling in love with." She nodded to the group of modern-day hippies who stood arm and arm. "I am thankful that I now have the craziest guardian angel." She tossed her rose into the ocean, then looking back, she saw Travis standing in the back.

After talking with several people, she suddenly realized that she hadn't explained to Finn anything about Travis. They both walked up to her at the same time.

"You did great." Finn put his arm around Sadie who shrugged with Travis standing next to him.

"Yes, you did," Travis said. Finn looked at him a little confused, obviously sensing the sudden tension. "And you must be the bartender." Travis stuck out his hand.

Finn slowly shook it. "Actually, the owner, but I do a little of everything." He looked at Sadie. "Do you know each other?"

The tension built immediately and both men stared at each other. Sadie began to say something but with the twenty-four hours of emotions, tiredness, and lack of water, she began feeling light-headed.

"You ok?" Finn caught her as she stumbled.

"Sadie." Travis grabbed her other arm.

"Who are you?" Finn pulled her up and away from Travis.

"I'm Travis," he said like Finn was supposed to know.

"Well, Travis. I have her. Thank you for stopping by."

"Stopping by? I came to get Sadie and to take Paige's body home."

B walked over with an empty tray from the restaurant in her hand. "Hold this." She slapped it in the chest of Travis and took Sadie from Finn. As they eased to the bar to sit, the men stood toe to toe with fists clinched and tempers at a boiling point.

"Finn, I need to. . ." Sadie started to say but a sudden thump of her heart skipping several beats silenced her words. Her body temperature shot through the roof and sweat immediately beaded up on her forehead. "B?" she mumbled.

"What, honey?"

"I. . ." Her body switched temperatures and a cold spell swept over her body. She last saw B standing over her and the two men in the background, the world spun uncontrollably and then silence.

***

"Hey!" Finn heard B yell. "Get the firemen!" She pointed to the crowd.

Both Finn and Travis jogged to Sadie who was lying on the sand. One of the firemen heard B and pulled another with him as they jogged over to see what was going on. "She just passed out. You two dumb-asses have picked a wrong time to start a cock fight."

One of the firemen leaned down to listen to her breathing then looked shocked at the other fireman. "Pulse?" he asked.

The other looked just as shocked. "No." Simultaneously they turned and yelled for the chief and the defibrillator. A couple other firemen and the chief quickly came to their calling and reassessed the situation. Without a word the chief ripped Sadie's shirt and placed the pads for the defibrillator.

Finn stood speechless and confused. "She really doesn't have a pulse?" He looked at Travis, then knelt beside her, wanting to touch her but the chief waved him back as he sent electricity bolting through her body. Her chest jumped with each press of the button.

"This isn't real." Finn couldn't make sense of it.

***

Sadie walked in a soft and quiet state wondering where she was, it was bright and warm and extremely peaceful. She had many dreams, but this was different—she couldn't place her finger on it but it was different. A figure came into view and walked toward her. There were many smiles she had witnessed in her time but this one was imprinted in her mind; a smile that met her when she woke in the mornings and a smile before going to bed at night. Her heart pounded uncontrollable as he approached her.

"Dad!"

fifty seven

Finn quickly closed the office door in the bar and made one last round throughout the bar. "I've got this." B stood at the end of the bar with a hand on her hip. The roar of twin turbo jet engines buzzed The Split and in a normal fashion banked to the right setting up for a landing. "Finn! Get your butt to Atlanta."

"Ok, I'm gone. I'll call you."

RK had the golf cart backed up and as soon as Finn jumped in, they took off toward the airport. It had been the longest eight hours of his life. The medivac that flew Sadie to Belize City only had room for one and that one person who took the seat was Travis. Finn had gotten word from a friend at the airport that they flew Sadie and Travis to Atlanta. Finn couldn't understand why Travis refused medical attention at the nearest hospital and still wasn't clear who he was and what authority he had. B had convinced Finn to let them go, since it seemed to be in the best interest for Sadie. All in the last eight hours.

In Finn's mind he wanted to put himself first, but if Sadie had a past with Travis, compared to their three and half weeks, then maybe for her best interest it was best for Travis to go with her.

The door shut on his father's jet with the captain's voice over the intercom announcing that they would be taking off and in Atlanta in less than three hours. Finn prepared himself for a controversial meeting with Travis. The thought of Sadie having different feelings for him wasn't even considered.

His cell phone rang with Julie's picture on the phone. "Hey, sis."

"How are you?"

"I'm good. Are you there?"

"I am and she's in stable condition. I'll have a car for you at the airport. Finn?" She paused on the phone "Who is this Travis guy?"

"I really don't know…ex-boyfriend maybe?"

"I don't want to start something that isn't true, but he has rights for her health. I don't want to alarm you… but I think he's her husband."

Finn thought for a moment. "Husband? That's absurd. She isn't married."

"Finn, what if he is?"

Thoughts flooded Finn's head about the three weeks they spent together and never once did she allude that she was even in a relationship, much less married. But little pieces started to surface and leaning back in the leather seat he suddenly realized he didn't know Sadie. *Why was she in the hospital and why did Travis know what was going on with her and I didn't? Holy crap, am I being played?* Before long Finn realized the severity of his three weeks. *How can you know someone in such a short time?*

His ears began popping, insinuating their altitude was dropping and that he'd be on Georgia ground soon. With Paige's death, Sadie's close call to death, and dealing with her husband or ex-husband weighing on his shoulders, he questioned rather to ask the pilot to take him back to Caulker. The ride to the hospital was long enough to create doubt in his head about the whole relationship with her. Traffic was as normal, backed up and stacked from the city to the outlining areas.

An hour and a half later the car dropped him off at the front doors to the hospital where Julie met him.

"Don't say anything, I just want to see Sadie," he said.

"That might not be as easy as you think. This Travis guy has the say of who gets to go back and see her. He didn't give me the time of day."

"Great."

They rode the elevator up to the fourth floor and stepped out onto the cardiac floor where the first face he saw was Travis. Finn walked toward him with the intentions of not taking no for an answer to see Sadie. "How is she?" he asked.

"She is good and asking for you."

"And you're not going to let me see her?"

Travis drew back. "Why would I not let you see her?"

"Who are you?" Finn barely keep his temper under control.

"I guess we never were introduced. Normally I would jack with you but considering the circumstance of losing Paige, I'll be honest with you."

"Gee, thanks," Finn answered sarcastically.

"I'm Sadie's last family member, her brother."

Brother? Damn I'm an idiot. "Sorry, I thought you were someone else."

Travis laughed. "I'm not her boyfriend. I don't recall her ever having one . . . until she went to Belize against my say-so. Not that I knew exactly where she went but–"

Finn felt he had some ground now that he knew who Travis was. "Not butting in family but why would she need your say-so?"

"She didn't tell you?"

"Tell me what?"

Travis's demeanor changed instantly along with his voice. "Sadie has a rare heart disease."

"What?" Finn answered. He felt all the blood drain from his face and his knees felt like jello.

"We lost our father to the same disease."

"But…but isn't heart disease treatable?" Finn asked feeling Julie grab his arm. "It is. It's *got* to be! I can't lose her." He looked at Julie then back to Travis.

"She has a condition that is linked to cardiac syndrome x. We have had the world's greatest doctors treating her case and even they don't know how to stop it. Her heart is dying."

"What?" Finn stated grasping the realization. "Dying? What do you mean dying? How long?"

"Nobody knows for sure. Dad lived a year longer than the doctors expected. Maybe I should

367

let her tell you." He stepped out of the way to the double doors that led back to an ICU cardiac area.

Finn let go of Julie and disappeared through the doors, where a nurse smiled as if she knew him. "Looking for Sadie?"

"I am."

"Come with me." She walked him down a long white hall to a door that wasn't completely closed. "Sadie? I think I found your knight and shining armor." She stepped out of his way. Finn walked into a room with instruments surrounding Sadie's bed.

"Not the greatest place to reunite with you, huh?" She smiled.

"I guess not."

She reached for his hand, but he stayed his distance as if he wasn't sure who she was anymore. "I understand if you're upset with me."

"Why didn't you tell me?"

"I guess I didn't want anyone to feel sorry for me. Plus, everything happened so fast. Please come here." She reached out again.

Finn walked closer to see that her eyes were darker, and her complexion was pale; she didn't look the same as when she walked in Drifters Reef.

She dropped her hand. "Now that you know, I understand if you leave." They stared at each other.

"I wish you have been truthful with me."

"I know, I'm sorry. There was never a good time to tell you I'm dying."

Finn stepped to her side and picked up her hand, her hand that had little circulation, so cold. "What do we do?" he asked.

She smiled. "You go back to Caye Caulker and make great beer. I am going to spend the little time I have right here."

"No, you can beat this. You can . . ."

She stopped him. "I can't. I wish there was a different way, but this is it. And it's ok. I have come to peace with it. The last three weeks with you in the most beautiful place in the world is the perfect ending."

"Don't say that."

"Finn, look at me. I never intended to lead you to believe that we were forever. But then I honestly bought in to it myself. But this is the truth, and this is my life—however long it is. It hurts, but the best thing for us is that you leave. Good bye Finn." She released his hand.

Tears formed in his eyes, joined by her tears and together they said their goodbyes without words. He kissed her one last time and turned to walk out never looking back.

370

Go Slow

fifty eight

The summer months turned to fall then to winter, and the weather on Caye Caulker changed a few degrees but for the most part stayed the same. Locals claimed that during winter months the sky would be clearer and the air cleaner but those that visited never could tell the difference. With winter, the tourist season slowed a bit, but the backpackers continued to visit the small island in search for the perfect sunset and the perfect motto: go slow.

The three people who worked the taxi dock never got in a hurry and seeing the green and yellow boat appear on the horizon, two of them shifted in their seats but the other never woke up. Two younger boys, who should have been in school, raced to meet the taxi pulling a wagon of bottle waters they were selling. One of them had a dozen blue stones wrapped in wire and attached to leather straps for necklaces. Caulker was the first stop before going to Ambergris Caye and not many

371

people got off here, but today a hand full of drifters stepped off the boat.

"Hey, mon! Get up!" the deckhand yelled at the worker sleeping on the dock who just waved him off. It was only drifters getting off and they normally didn't have luggage, just their packs strapped to their shoulders. The boat never even tied off and the two young boys tried to peddle their water but only one of the backpackers bought a bottle.

A woman from Atlanta.

With a straw hat, aviator sunglass, and a gray backpack, Sadie opened the bottle of water and took a deep swig. Two of the other drifters joined her at the end of the dock. "So, this is where we say goodbye?"

"Yea, I believe so. Thanks for letting me island hop with you guys for the last few weeks."

"You are one cool gal; if things don't work out, we'll be at a hostel just south of here."

"I know of it." She smiled. They hugged and then went their separate ways.

Pulling her hat down tighter to keep from blowing off with a strong eastern wind she started walking down the beach road and past the surf shop. Toby and Shar were in the middle of teaching a

Go Slow

group of tourists how to paddle board before taking them out. She gave a gentle nod, but they never looked up.

Picking up her pace she walked out onto the main road and walked north. The street vendors worked the crowd doing their best to sell the trinkets and seashells, along with the food vendors who lofted aromas of lobster and fish. She gracefully waved a *no thank you* and continued up the road to the most known spot on the island, The Split.

Kicking sand as she walked, she made it to her final destination, a place and a journey that started six weeks earlier with a group she had met in Atlanta. The past six weeks had been a spiritual quest to ready herself for a commitment she was preparing for and a lifestyle change that had been inspired by her best friend.

In front of her was Drifters Reef. Sadie walked up to the bar.

"What'll you have?" B asked obviously not recognizing her through a straw hat and sunglasses.

Sadie lowered her glass. "A cold beer and maybe a hug?"

B froze and just stared as if she had witnessed a ghost walking up. "It'll be three dollars for the beer. I don't do hugs." She slid a can down the wooden bar.

Sadie had figured that she would have some animosity with some of the people. She hadn't been on the island since they airlifted her five months ago. "I like the can." She smiled at her creation.

"I tried to get him to change it, but he said he didn't have the time." B went to wiping off the counter with a white rag that had been draped over her shoulder.

The cold beer felt amazing to Sadie's lips and after a couple of swigs she focused back on B. "I'm sorry, B. I should have been in contact with you."

"You think?" B snapped back. "But I guess you have an excuse. Why not, all of your generation does."

Sadie wanted to continue to smooth things over, but she was there to see one person. "Is he around?"

Without looking up from the bar. "He stayed for three weeks after he got back from Atlanta."

"Stayed?"

"Sold me the bar and gave his brewery to his father." She looked up at her. "He fixed that damn boat of his and sailed away to start a new life. I thought he had a pretty damn good life here." She went back to wiping the bar.

Sadie's heart and stomach sunk, she had fought with her thoughts to call him, but with doctors and her brother arguing with her and treatment, she just broke free and left Georgia to clear her head. Never in a million years did she think Finn would leave too.

"B . . . I didn't know that . . ."

B threw the white rag at her. "I'll tell you what you didn't know! You bring your pretty little ass in here and win over one of the greatest guys. And then what? You don't tell him that you're dying! Instead you die here on this beach only to be brought back to life and then what? You run him out of the hospital and run him out of your life! If that ain't some crap then I don't know what is!"

Tears welled up in Sadie's eyes. "I didn't . . ."

"It wasn't just him you ran out on. There are a lot of people here that fell in love with you." She picked up another rag and started cleaning again.

Fully crying, "I'm sorry, B. I didn't know, I didn't know."

"Didn't know what?" B squared up to her with a hand on her hip.

Facing off with her, "I didn't know God was going to give me a miracle! You don't know how much praying I have done and how much begging I have done for an extra year, an extra month, or even a week!" She picked up the rag that B had thrown at her and set it on the bar. "I didn't come here five months ago to fall in love, I came here five months ago to die. But all that begging and praying I did . . . God didn't give me time, he gave me Finn. I was just too stupid to realize it until the day I asked him to leave the hospital. By then I thought it was too late." She sat on the bar stool. "Hell! I'm still screwing up."

B took a deep breath and shook her head. "Damn I hate millennials." She walked around the bar and pulled Sadie into her, hugging her like a mother would when their child is hurting. "What took you so long to get back here?"

With her head sunk in B's shoulder, "I took time to make Paige's dream come true before coming to get my dream. Now, I'm too late."

B pulled her back to face her. "Don't cry! I haven't been exactly honest . . ."

fifty nine

With her gray backpack strapped to her shoulder, Sadie walked up to a clean and sparkling boat with a freshly painted name on the back, *Go Slow*. The back door slid open and Finn stepped out without a shirt and carrying a handful of wires. He glanced in Sadie's direction, obviously not recognizing her through sunglasses and a straw hat, and made his way to the bridge. Halfway up the ladder he froze. Then looked over his shoulder.

"I see you named her." Sadie smiled.

"Someone told me it was bad luck to have a boat without a name."

She laughed. "Smart person."

He climbed down and set the wires on the deck. "What brings you to our little island?"

"You going somewhere?" She changed the question.

"Maybe."

Sadie approached the boat with a different reaction. "I'm sorry, Finn."

"You had to do what was best for you."

"And that is what almost cost me my life."

"So, you came here . . . for what?"

The sun started its trek into the horizon, displaying a show that Caye Caulker was known for. Sadie hadn't rehearsed what she was going to say to Finn; she had been praying he would accept her back, but their conversation wasn't going as she had hoped.

"I am not sure about miracles. My brother thinks that I am a walking miracle because I have proved all the doctors wrong. I do know that I have been asking for one for several years now. It was *time* that I was always asking for. But I never received it, instead you came along." She stepped onto the boat. "I don't know how long I am going to be here, but I do know the time I have I want to spend it with you."

Finn took both her hands in his. "I have been thinking about this and here's what I've come up with. I don't want to count the days that I don't have with you, I want to count the days I have with you."

Go Slow

Tears fill her eyes. "So, where does that leave us?"

"Together." He pressed his lips to hers.

"You still haven't answered my question."

"What's that?" He leaned back.

"Where you going?" She pointed to a clean boat with new engines.

Tipping her chin up with his finger, he smiled. "I was coming to get you."

380

Go Slow

Other books written by Lee DuCote